BOOK 1

A.G. WYATT

Copyright © 2014 by A.G. Wyatt

All rights reserved. No part of this book may be reproduced or transmitted in any form or by any means (including without limitation electronic, digital, optical, mechanical, photocopying, printing, recording, or otherwise), without the prior written permission of the author and the publisher.

All trademarks and brands referred to in this book are for illustrative purposes only, are the property of their respective owners and not affiliated with this publication in any way. Any trademarks being used without permission, and the publication of the trademark is not authorized by, associated with, or sponsored by the trademark owner.

Cover art: MadHouse

Icons: MotoTsume

Editing: Bridgette O'Hare

ISBN: 978-1505391718

CONTENTS

1	A Rustling in the Trees	1
2	Distant Company	9
3	Dumpsville	16
4	What Passes for Civilization	24
5	A Place of Safety	30
6	Beauty and a Beating	38
7	Making Friends	46
8	Living in Hope	53
9	Chain Gang	61
10	A Helping Hand	69
11	Last Night	77
12	Small Worlds	85
13	Blood	93
14	Amidst the Ruins	100

15	Going to Town	107
16	Tagging Along	113
17	Fight the Good Fight	122
18	Fight or Flight	128
19	Applied Intelligence	135
20	The Hunting Party	144
21	Kill or Be Killed	152
22	Last Gasp	161
23	After the Deluge	169
24	Something More Beside You	176
25	Or Should I Go?	184
26	The Elders	191
27	Noah's Choice	198
28	Believing	204

Chapter 1
A Rustling in the Trees

Noah woke with a start, one hand going for his revolver and the other for the ground beneath him, fumbling in the dark for a reminder of where he was. Even before he'd registered the feel of bark beneath his fingers, the sight of leaves all around clued him into where he was.

He paused, Bourne half-way out of its holster, and listened for what had torn him from his sleep. Not another meteorite crashing down into the woods. That noise would still be ringing in his ears and all the way down the valley for that matter. No, this was something softer, more subtle.

Right hand still resting on Bourne's handle, Noah carefully started unfastening the straps used to tie himself to the tree. Years ago he'd fastened himself in place with all sorts of ropes and haphazard knots, but not after the forest fire back in Tennessee that left his skin dappled by scars. Embers had flown at him on the wind as flames erupted through undergrowth dried out by one long damn summer. The tree beneath him had charred and twisted as he struggled to get loose of his self-imposed restraints. Now pale patches of flesh on his arm and around the older scar on his chest reminded him of the lesson learned.

He paused. It rustled again. A crackling in the treetops, something or someone coming towards him.

He unfastened the last strap, grabbed the branch above

him and hauled himself to his feet. The branch beneath him was sturdy, but still sagged a little as he shifted his weight.

By now he had Bourne unholstered. A glint off the revolver's well-oiled body reflected the light of the stars, or of the debris belt that glowed across the southern stretch of sky. Between the rippling leaves the belt appeared even more fractured than usual, a dapple of light against the midnight sky, a haze where the moon had once been.

The rustling came closer. Noah raised Bourne, clicked back the hammer. Of course, there weren't no bullets in the chamber, but whoever was coming didn't know that. Better hollow threats than no threats at all out here where the wild things roamed.

Even better than threats was not being seen. Noah drew himself against the tree, a knot pressing into his back as he descended into the deepest shadows. Movement now accompanied the approach of his unwelcomed company, a body swinging slowly but confidently through the foliage, pausing every few branches to look around for threats. As it leapt from one treetop to another, Noah caught a glimpse of gray-brown fur and long teeth. He swallowed, stayed calm. Up close he'd stand little chance against something so confident in the treetops. He was a hell of a climber, but even he couldn't swing from branch to branch like that. And those teeth... If this was some kind of maniac dressed in furs and ferocity, then he'd be cannibal chow long before he reached the ground.

The stranger reached the tree-top opposite Noah and paused. A shadow against the dimly lit trunk of the tree, Noah could make out its head turning from side to side. Then it stopped, hunched suddenly forward and prowled along the branch. It emerged from the shadows, staring straight at him with beady red eyes.

Noah almost laughed. A baboon. A long-faced, big-assed

baboon. Then it bared its teeth and hissed at him, and the humor drained away. Weird as it was to see a baboon swinging through rural Virginia, up close a baboon stopped being funny and became a wide barrel chest, long strong fingers and deadly looking teeth. What did baboons eat? Were they carnivores? Was it cannibalism if an animal ate a human?

He raised Bourne more confidently, pointed the gun straight at the baboon's face and hoped it had seen one before. It paused, then made a strange rasping sound.

Was a damned baboon laughing at him?

Noah thought about how he must look and almost burst out laughing himself. A human, one of nature's lousiest climbers despite all his years in the wild, dangling from a tree branch like some kid on a rope swing, dressed in patched jeans and a raggedy old coat, his beard as wild as his hair, waving a revolver that didn't even hold the threat of bullets. Man, once the master of the Earth, nothing more than supper for a ridiculous damned ape.

Worse, not even worthy of being supper for an ape. The baboon turned, exposing its big bare ass to Noah like a final insult, and swung away through the trees.

Noah sagged, all the tension draining out of him, and settled back onto his branch. He holstered Bourne and one by one began fastening the buckles on his harness.

Strangest damn thing, he thought, a baboon wild in Virginia. Then he looked down at his harness and back up at the pale, hazy band splitting the darkness of the sky.

Maybe not the strangest thing. Not by any sane standard.

The next day Noah awoke with the dawn, the only alarm clock he needed...even before the world had fallen apart. At least some things remained the same. He knew some folks considered the way the world was to be a blessing, folks who might be surprised he was not one of them. After all, he had always been an outdoors kind of guy raised on hunting, fishing, and trekking in the wild. Turned out to be a lot less fun when you didn't have a bottle of whiskey for around the campfire, a soft bed at the end of it, or central heating when winter came.

If winter decided to come this time around.

He pulled a cloth pouch from his coat pocket, opened it and tore a strip of jerky from the lump inside. A trade from a farmer out west, a man who had somehow hung on to a small herd of cattle through the past twenty years. It wasn't the best jerky Noah had ever tasted, but it was the best thing he had on him and he chewed it with relish, the salt flavor making his mouth water.

While he chewed, he looked around, checking for threats and regaining his bearings. No sign of the baboon from the previous night, and the only critter moving along the forest floor was a rabbit. That was a good sign, maybe there would be something in his snares. Maybe he would have fresh meat tonight.

He unbuckled himself from the harness, untied it from the tree, then opened his rucksack and carefully stowed the collection of straps and ropes away inside. After untying the bag itself, he settled it over his shoulders. Having checked that Bourne was securely in place, he took one more look around and scrambled down the tree.

Not many people, or animals, came through this part of the forest. Leaf mulch had gone undisturbed all winter, slowly rotting into the ground, leaving a soft surface that put a spring in his step. Violets and dandelions poked their heads through the rotting mulch, bright blues and yellows amid the spring greenery breaking out all around. He had never been much for flowers, but seeing them now gave him a little hope, and wasn't life meant to bring hope?

All Noah hoped for was to find something decent to scavenge in the stores down the highway, maybe canned food that had lasted or some meds.

He took a quick lap through the surrounding trees, retrieving his snares from the previous night. Two held rabbits, which he dropped into a tow sack tied to his belt. He'd deal with the skinning later, for now he kept the fur on, packaging wrapped around meat from God's own grocery store.

They had been called grocery stores, right? Noah thought so, but childhood memories were fading, and a man's recollections could get hazy out here on his own.

"Course I ain't ever alone when I've got you," he said, patting Bourne.

He pulled a cluster of dandelions and added the leaves to his sack. Greens to help keep his body together. They were still young and tender as they should be at this stage of growth - not that you ever knew when you'd find them anymore, seeing as the seasons were shot to hell and the weather with them.

A stream nearby was a bonus, the water running fresh and clear. The broken outline of his reflection stared back as he stooped to drink. The beard was almost ZZ Top caliber now, long and pointed, though dark like the rest of his hair. It showed less age than his skin. Worn and leathery hands, like he'd borrowed off some old man, scooped up the water. He drank deeply, sighing with satisfaction at the crisp, clear taste, then filled his canteens for later.

Half a mile north of the tree he had spent the night in, Noah found the highway again. The signs had all been ripped up for their metal years ago, but he guessed from an old map he'd found in a car that it was 81. The highway number mattered far less than what he could scavenge along the route. But he figured if he kept following this one north-east, it should take him to the towns around D.C. full of old deserted shops and fancy houses. Maybe, if he got lucky, he would find some government building or long abandoned supply depot, the jackpot for any scavenging nomad. Somewhere with blankets and medicine, canned goods still edible after twenty years, water bottles, new pants, bullets even…

So busy dreaming of what he might find, he almost stepped out of the woods and onto the broken asphalt. A wagon or horse on the road might be exposed, but at least it was moving fast. A man, trudging mile after mile out in the open for all to see, that man was just asking for trouble.

Keeping the road in sight, Noah walked through the woods south of the highway. The remnants of a wreck caught his attention. Two cars that had long ago collided, then later been dragged off by some good citizen keeping the roads clear or maybe just some convoy doing what was needed so they could keep moving. Either way, the cars had been there long enough for the soot to wash away and be replaced by rust.

Noah crawled inside the more intact car, rummaging around in the floorboard and glove compartment. But all he found was rabbit droppings, charred bones and the dead plastic brick of a slightly melted reading tablet. In the early wilderness days he might have gotten his hopes up with a thing like that, thinking about all the books he could read on these dark, lonely nights. He'd learned his lesson. Even if he could have found a power supply, the tablet would have been fried when the moon exploded, just like every other electronic device on the planet.

Another flash blazed across the sky and a meteorite crashed into the hills to the west. It hadn't even been a dot on the distant horizon when he arrived, and there was no good reason to delay like that. Time to get moving again.

An intense, dry heat made the air fizz off the road and sweat run down Noah's back. His exposed skin roasted, as if he weren't already well browned and weather wrinkled enough. He'd taken off his coat, leaving his stained, frayed shirt exposed to the air, but still his body wept at the heat.

He paused before the overpass. Places like this could be dangerous. Worse if you were traveling the road underneath, unable to see who might be lurking above, ready to leap out on you. Bandits or local militias or worse. But even from his perspective traveling over the top, it was an exposed place to be. It hung above the road below, a raised, open space that offered no shelter and no place to hide. You could be seen for miles in either direction.

Pausing in the woods overlooking the overpass, he gathered old dried leaves and sticks, carefully arranged them in a sheltered spot and used flint and steel to start a fire. He skinned the rabbits and set them to roasting, all the while watching the road. There were risks in lighting a fire when there might be other people hidden nearby, but it was better than doing it wherever he stayed the night. If there were ambushers, maybe this would draw them out.

An hour later the only thing that had moved was the sun, creeping across the empty blue heavens. Noah sucked the last juices from the first rabbit's bones, stowed the second in his sack and kicked dirt over the fire. The overpass was clear as it would ever be.

One last look around and Noah walked out of the woods, onto the road, and towards the overpass. He moved on, well rested after his break, feet ready rather than weary. But tension knotted his gut. He strode as fast as he could along the highway, past another overturned car and towards the midway point.

A roar exploded from the road off to his left and Noah leapt back into cover behind the car.

In the distance, something was tearing down the other highway out of the north, heading straight towards the overpass.

Someone was coming.

CHAPTER 2
DISTANT COMPANY

Someone turned out to be an understatement. As Noah watched from behind the car, the sound of motorbikes roared out of the distance and down the highway. They skirted around a line of abandoned cars just before the overpass, the riders shouting to each other. One turned back while the other continued down the road. Noah watched the half skull painted across the back of his old biker leathers fade as he disappeared into the south.

The bikes were barely out of sight when another vehicle appeared, bigger and louder, grumbling its way from the north like it had suffered years of abuse by a harsh world and harsher home-brewed fuel. The red blob appearing around the bend emerged into view as a tow truck, windows covered with wire grills and metal plates, three passengers hanging onto the winch at the back. The first biker was with them, gesturing again at the blockage in the road, but he roared on beneath the overpass while the truck and its crew stopped and began clearing the road.

Outliers, Noah thought. Scouts clearing the way for a larger group.

He considered making a run for the trees. They weren't looking his way, but there was always a chance they might see him if he ran. They might not be concerned about strangers who kept themselves to themselves. Or they might. Certainly he had no interest in a confrontation with these people, much less talking with them. He hadn't seen a soul in weeks, and he liked it that way.

There was no rush – after all, Washington was just one more foraging ground across the wilderness that had once been America. What waited for him there could wait another day.

Cramps began to grip the muscles of Noah's legs. He knew he was going to be immobile for a while and needed to make himself comfortable.

Waiting until he was sure the truck crew was preoccupied, he opened the door of the car concealing him just enough to ease himself inside. The car had clearly been there a while, but the seats were mostly intact. He settled into the least moldy one, sinking far enough that he could watch the road without being seen. Then he waited.

By the time the truck crew cleared the cars from the road below him, the rest of their convoy had arrived. A full nomadic community, maybe forty vehicles in all shapes and sizes, from a battered old school bus spewing steam from its ragged bonnet to a couple of dozen horse drawn carts, then followed up by bicycles and even a couple of women taking turns to push a wheelbarrow. The motorbikes were clearly the cream of the crop, but it was quite a harvest of wheeled vehicles.

Noah watched the ramshackle community with a sense of detached curiosity. The people were as mixed as the vehicles, from a gray-haired black guy in dungarees who seemed to be in charge of the group, to a blend of folks around Noah's age, down to kids who could never have known the world as it once was.

A couple of teenagers were rough-housing by the side of the road – a dark haired girl shoving her younger brother around while they waited to move on. It reminded Noah of when he'd been that younger brother, and a pang of loss for Jeb and Pete tugged at his chest. Not just for the early days on the road when they'd kept him going through the mind-numbing loss of everything they'd known, but for the times when they'd been young and naive and had the whole world at their feet.

More naive than they'd ever known. But then who could have seen this coming?

Just thinking about those times made him want a smoke. He reached for the packet in his top left pocket and the three precious, stale, old cigarettes it still contained. He stopped himself before he'd even got one out. There were people nearby, people whose attention he didn't want.

He chewed on a strip of jerky to distract himself and watched the caravan.

They were moving again, through the gap between the cars and down the solid strip of highway that remained despite the weeds clawing their way in from the edges. The gray-haired leader looked up as he passed by below. Noah sank deeper into his seat, tensed as he listened for any sign they'd spotted him.

Instead, the cough and splutter of engines, the clopping of hooves, and the rumble of wheels on tarmac filled the air.

As the noise faded, Noah rose in his seat and looked again at the mass of machinery disappearing down the highway. The two teenagers he had watched romped at the back, helping a red-headed woman in a patched green dress push her wheelbarrow along. The boy finally got revenge on his sister, punching her in the arm while she was busy pushing the barrow, then looking all innocent when the woman turned to see what the fuss was about. As the girl protested to an indifferent authority, Noah found himself chuckling.

He looked up the road north-east, then back towards the

column disappearing south. Sure he didn't much like people, but it had been a long time since he'd had any entertainment.

"Y'know what?" he murmured, patting Bourne as he opened the car door. "Washington can wait."

Noah followed the assembly at a distance for the next few days. It was easy to do - the scouts were mostly occupied seeing what was ahead rather than what lay behind, and when they did double back he just drew back deeper into the woods. Walking through woods was a skill, and one he had plenty of practice at. Keeping up with a group traveling at the speed of a wheelbarrow wasn't much of a challenge.

By the third night he was getting close enough under cover of darkness that he could overhear brief snatches of conversation, at least when the speakers were getting loud. He tried to maneuver himself so that he could watch Sally and Todd, the teenagers he'd spotted on the first day, as well as Mary and Claudette, the women who shared wheelbarrow duties with them. It was easy enough to do - wherever the group camped they ended up near the edge, away from the warmth and loud conversations that went on around the central campfire. Their place was out near the shadows, almost as much as Noah's was.

That third night the little community reminded Noah of what people were really like.

Tyrone, the group's gray-haired leader, called them all together after dinner. He pointed to a map stuck against the side of the bus, an old, frayed thing showing the roads as they had been before all Hell hit. The gathering was too close to the center of camp for Noah to hear what was being said, but it looked like Tyrone had made a decision between two roads.

Only, not everybody was happy with Tyrone's choice. One of the motorbike riders – the one Noah thought of as Half-Skull for the symbol on his jacket – stepped forward and gestured angrily towards Tyrone. Some seemed to be trying to shout him down, while others stood behind him, arms folded, glaring at the rest.

Tyrone argued back. Angry words turned to angry gestures, turned to Half-Skull shoving Tyrone and Tyrone shoving him back. Something glittered in Half-Skull's hand as he slammed into the older man.

Tyrone sank to his knees, hands clutching at a knife handle protruding from his chest.

The whole community fell silent as they watched their leader stare in shock at Half-Skull and then topple over in a pool of blood.

Someone screamed, then was silenced by a gesture from one of Half-Skull's friends.

There was no loud banter around the campfire that night. Sally and Todd huddled together in their blankets, not arguing or fighting, but clinging to each other with fierce protectiveness.

Noah remembered Jeb and Pete again, remembered the way he'd clung to them when things went bad, and how on the worst off all mornings that had left him soaked through with their blood.

He smoked a cigarette.

The next day the group moved on, but the atmosphere was different. Half-Skull stood on top of the bus as it rumbled along, watching the people around him as much as he watched the road ahead. Heads were lowered, shoulders slumped. The group had always seemed like a fragile band, undernourished and riddled with disease, half of them hobbling or blighted by sores and hacking coughs. But Noah had never seen them so downtrodden.

Watching them no longer lifted his spirits. And yet he could not help following, drawn along by some terrible compulsion. Did he want to keep seeing people, or did he just want to know what would happen next? He asked Bourne, but his holstered companion remained silent.

Their next stop was a junction where the highway met another road running east to west. An old gas station seemed to be the reason for the stop. Half-Skull set people to work retrieving any dregs of fuel still remaining in its tanks. Noah figured it for a lost cause. They weren't far enough into the wilds for such a place not to have been thoroughly ransacked, but he watched with the same hollow, edgy feeling he'd watched everything else since Tyrone's death.

Tyrone had seemed like a good man, as much as such people still existed. Half-Skull wasn't. He and his allies prowled the camp, most of them carrying muskets, while the others worked. If they were meant to be guarding against outside dangers, then they were looking the wrong way. It crossed Noah's mind that was to his advantage, as they might not have viewed him with friendly eyes. The thought didn't reassure him none.

He was watching Sally and Todd cook the company's dinner, their usual arguments reduced to whispers, when a scream echoed through the camp. His hand went straight for Bourne, his eyes and everybody else's following the sound to the darkness at the edge of the camp.

Half-Skull had a handful of Mary the wheelbarrow wrangler's red hair. He yanked her head to one side as he pushed her against a wagon and wrenched up her skirts. She screamed and battered futilely against his chest, her face contorted in horrified panic. Half-Skull's fist collided with the side of her face, leaving a trickle of blood in its wake, then he turned his glare on the rest of the camp.

Sally stood but was pulled back down by Todd. Everyone else turned away except for Half-Skull's gang, several of whom were grinning with approval at their leader.

Mary's screams turned to sobs as Half-Skull tore her dress entirely away.

Noah turned away, too. His hand wrapped around Bourne's handle, gripping so tightly his fingers went cold. Bourne who was empty of bullets, unlike those muskets in the camp. Bourne, who made him feel so powerful in his idle moments, now left him impotent in the face of depravity. But, then, he didn't know the woman. She didn't even know he existed. Why would he risk anything for her when her own people wouldn't?

His stomach tightened. These people sickened him, just like most did in the end. Better to be alone than constantly reminded of what humanity really was.

He picked up his pack, drew deeper into the shelter of the trees, and started walking east.

CHAPTER 3
DUMPSVILLE

A FEW DAYS LATER Noah found the town of Dumpsville lying an hour's trek north of the highway. For the first time in a month, he thought he might finally scavenge some decent supplies. The journey east so far had been bitterly disappointing – a few empty houses and a burned-down gas station, and only one rabbit in his snares. Even the local mushrooms had an unhealthy purple color that no sane man would put in his mouth. But Dumpsville held real promise, as much as anything made by people could.

It probably had a proper name once, something sweet and homey to fit its cozy, secluded setting. Cherry Wood, maybe? Or Pastor Heights. Something that spoke of family values and the Appalachian country spirit. But the meteorite that had hit the road at the southern end of town had taken out whatever welcome sign had proudly declared its name, and so Noah filled the gap. He hated towns like Dumpsville – they reminded him too much of home.

He skirted around the edge of the meteorite crater. It had been there a while, long enough for a whole range of plants to sprout up in the rubble, including clusters of those purple mushrooms and even some small trees. Which probably meant no-one had been around for a long time either, otherwise they would have done something to repair the road. Maybe the inhabitants had evacuated in the early days, headed to somewhere more secure and populous, and never returned. Maybe they'd taken the meteorite as a sign from the heavens and pulled up stakes to move on – all it took was one charismatic preacher and a couple of misfortunes to poison people's judgment. Or maybe they'd just decided it wasn't worth staying with the main road in ruins. Could be they were all dead now, or living on some Caribbean island like the characters in a pre-collapse holiday brochure. Whatever the case, Dumpsville seemed both deserted and largely untouched, the best sort of town.

Noah walked Main Street, past squat houses with big yards and a couple of boxy shops. His heart leapt at the sight of a gun store, a grin splitting his face at the thought of such a place long left untouched. It only took a moment's work to bust the lock and get inside.

Once inside, his heart sank. The store had been thoroughly and neatly cleaned out. Not a gun on the walls, not a bullet on the shelves, just a pile of crumbling paper targets and a counter gray with years of dust. Whatever their motives, the townspeople had gone fully armed when they left. Even after pillaging through the backs of cupboards and in a store room behind the register, Noah came up empty handed. Finding ammunition was looking a whole heap less likely for Noah.

"Sorry buddy." He patted Bourne. "Guess you're going hungry tonight."

"That's 'cause you're in the wrong shop bro."

Noah spun around at the sound of the voice, Bourne out of his holster and pointed towards the stranger silhouetted in the doorway.

"Whoa, chill!" The guy's hands flew into the air and he took two careful steps back into the street. Daylight revealed a grin through his ragged blond beard despite having a gun trained on him. "No need for that. There's a Walmart down the street, got more food than both of us can carry."

Noah cautiously lowered Bourne. He wasn't in the mood for more people, and he liked surprises the same way a rodeo bull liked a rider on his back. But if this guy had meant him harm then he'd wasted his best opportunity, which made him friendly or stupid, and either way Noah could handle him.

He slid Bourne back into his holster.

"What's your name?" Noah asked.

"Paul." The other guy lowered his hands, held one out in greeting. "Nice to meet you, bro."

Paul didn't know the town's name any more than Noah did, and he laughed heartily at the idea of *Dumpsville*. But then, Paul laughed heartily at most things.

"You should save that one for New York bro." Paul brushed a dollop of sauce from his faded letterman jacket and leaned back in his plastic chair, reaching to open another can of beans. "Place is a total wreck. There's, like, old cars jamming up half the streets, skyscrapers with all the windows smashed out, all kinds of crazy shit. Capital of the world, take away the computers and it's nothing but dead concrete. I mean seriously, it makes total sense man. What can you grow in New York, huh? Am I right?"

His face contorted as he tasted the beans, cast that can aside and reached for another. The can clattered to the curb, spilling its contents across the Walmart parking lot.

"Thought this shit would last forever," he continued. "Like cockroaches or this rash I caught off some skanky cheerleader in college. I swear to God, you do not want to know what that did to Big Paul. Every minute was like some eternity of torment. I may not believe in Jesus, but I totally believe in penicillin."

After a pause he spoke again.

"Wonder if they still make penicillin."

A flash accompanied by a growing roar announced the arrival of a meteorite. Blazing a long, glowing path through the air above Dumpsville, it turned the sky from blue to a burning orange before crashing into a nearby hillside, the explosion echoing through the valley.

"You think that's it?" Paul asked, looking up to see if any more fragments would follow.

"Reckon so." Noah watched the woods where the meteorite had hit. If a fire broke out, it could make it risky to keep heading east. But though the crater smoldered, there was no sign of flames.

"What about you man?" Paul asked. "Where you from? Where you going? What's your place in this crazy, mixed up life on the road?"

Noah hesitated. He'd known Paul for all of an hour, though he'd heard enough of his stories to fill in a lifetime. But then what was there to lose? And how else could you get news of the road ahead, if not by sharing with other wanderers?

Still, his hand drifted a little towards Bourne as he leaned back, a half-empty can of spaghetti resting on his full belly, and considered where to start.

"I grew up in Tennessee," he said at last. "No place you would've heard of. I was barely eighteen when all of this happened." He waved his hand, taking in the deserted buildings and the dust rising from the fresh crater in the distance. "Been working odd jobs - construction, auto, all kinds of stuff with my hands. I was fixing to settle down and be another small town nobody, huntin' and fishin' on the weekends, marrying some girl I'd known since she was wearing her hair in pigtails.

"If it wasn't for my older brothers I'd likely have died. We stayed in town, but a new mayor took over and that place clean went to Hell. Jeb and Pete, they tried to stand up to him, but he didn't like that. He..."

The words caught in Noah's throat, swollen by the horror of memory. Of waking into their shared room one morning to see Jeb's blood-soaked sheets, rushing over to shake Pete awake but finding him cold and pale as a midwinter snow, his throat sliced open, eyes wide and staring up at Noah, demanding justice.

For an hour he'd just sat there, rocking back and forth on the blood-soaked floor, unable to comprehend what he'd seen, even more bewildered to still be alive. At last he'd pulled himself together enough to pull out Jeb's stash and roll the fattest, strongest joint he'd ever seen. As the glow crackled up the bloodstained paper and fragrant smoke filled his lungs, Noah had tried to make sense of it all. Why the killing was obvious. Gunderson had had it in for Jeb and Pete for weeks. But why leave Noah? Had the self-proclaimed mayor forgotten about him? Had he or his lackeys not seen him in the darkness? Maybe they just thought he wasn't a threat, or found it funny to leave him alive and suffering, a reminder that they could bring anybody to their knees.

Nobody brought the Brennan boys to their knees.

That night Noah took Pete's knife and paid a return visit to the apartment above town hall.

The flash of another meteorite brought Noah back to the present. He lit a cigarette from one of the packs they'd found behind the counter, passed another to Paul.

"Let's just say it ended badly," he said as last. "And he won't be troubling folks no more. But after that, I couldn't stick around. It wasn't just that I was afraid of what I might face for my revenge, I s'pose I was more afraid of living in that town and seeing those streets but not my brothers walking them, than I was of dying there."

"Been on the road ever since - half a lifetime and more, but I've never looked back."

Paul nodded sagely.

"That's some heavy shit, bro," he said at last. "Some major heavy shit."

"No worse than most folks by now, I expect." Noah took a long drag on his cigarette, fought down the sorrow that rose within him, threatening to steal away his energy, his will to go on. He flicked the butt away, lit another, looked for a distraction. "What's next for you?"

"Heading south, catch me some sunshine," Paul said. "Winter was hella cold upstate this year. I want to get somewhere hot before I lose any more of these bad boys." He pulled off one of his boots, revealing the blackened stumps of two toes eaten away by frostbite.

"Hate to tell you this," Noah said, "but it ain't gonna be much better down south. Weather's a mess wherever you go. Even the Bayou gets frozen some winters now. And before that, you'll have to bake through the summer - from here on out it gets hotter every day."

"Thanks for the warning bro." Paul pulled his sock and shoe back on, started tying the twine that had replaced the laces. "But what I saw this winter, storms burying whole houses in snow, fucking polar bears roaming the streets, whatever's down south it can't be any worse. What about you? Where next for Tennessee's own Lone Ranger?"

"Keep heading east. See what I can find."

Paul gave his thoughtful nod of the head. He had a way of gazing off into the distance that made him look wise until you heard him speak. It was only then that the distance and the pauses were revealed as vacancy, not thoughtfulness. There was far worse company to be had, but he wasn't exactly filling Noah with a desire for civilization.

"Maybe two hours of daylight left," Paul said. "Trade before we part?"

Noah nodded. It was the common parting point for folks on the road, getting the chance to switch supplies before going their separate ways, not giving the other guy time to plan a scam or rob you of the wealth you'd shown them.

"You got any bullets?" Noah asked.

"Sorry bro." Paul shook his head. "No-one left that shit lying around. Got this though."

He pulled a bottle of brown liquid out of his pack, the remnants of a whiskey label still visible across the middle. Noah grinned, then sagged as he realized how little he had to trade.

"Nothing I'd love more," he said, and he could hear the longing in his own voice. "But all I've got are these."

He undid a tow sack hanging off of his backpack, opened it up to reveal the rabbit skins inside.

Paul grinned.

"Shit man, that is badass," he said, gazing into the bag. "I saw some needle and thread back in the store. Can make me a proper fur coat, like some crazy wild man out of history. I'm gonna be mother-fucking Captain Caveman."

Noah blinked in confusion. Was this guy for real? How had he lasted this long if he couldn't even trap and skin his own food?

But then he remembered the baboon. The world was a crazy place, best not to question the good bits of that craziness.

"You're a good dude, Noah," Paul said, handing over the bottle. "You travel safe, you hear?"

Noah couldn't remember the last time he'd had the chance to get properly, wretchedly drunk. That night he managed, screaming at the crazy world long into the night, passing out at last in a patch of tall grass. He woke the next morning wrapped around his precious, empty whiskey bottle, his thoughts wrapped around a kernel of fierce pain.

He got up, tried to brush the dew from his clothes, and walked on alone.

CHAPTER 4
WHAT PASSES FOR CIVILIZATION

When spring-like weather rolled through, it was a good time to be heading to higher ground. As the snow and storms eased off, the prospect of ascending into the Appalachians became more practical, with less threat of snow or violent storms to rip Noah off a hillside and leave him lying like a broken doll in the valley below.

There were times he cursed his own overactive imagination. This was one of those times.

The advantage of heading up the mountain was the pickings to be had now that the weather was changing. As animals emerged from hibernation and dormant plants started to appear, suddenly a wealth of eating could be found, as great a bounty as he'd see before the fall came. And as Dumpsville had reminded him, up here there were plenty of places that had been abandoned early on that other drifters might not have completely emptied out. One more reason to get up the mountain quickly, before anybody else did.

The next place he found had once been like Dumpsville, but time, humanity and the ravages of a devastating climate had entirely transformed it. The houses were ruins at best, burned out shells at worst. Tree roots and meteorite falls had turned the roads into little more than broken clumps of asphalt between raised ridges of dirt. There were plenty of stores, but those that still stood had been thoroughly looted, windows smashed in, shelves not just emptied but torn down and scattered across the grimy floors.

'So this is what passes for civilization around here,' he muttered to Bourne as he walked past the rusted remains of a children's playground and on towards what appeared to be a high school.

The stores might be empty, but there were always opportunities for a wanderer who knew where to look. Community centers, if they could be found, sometimes had a stockpile of emergency blankets and old dried food for the homeless. If you could break through the reinforced doors then town hall emergency shelters sometimes held secret stashes, as rare and as precious as toilet paper in an abandoned outhouse. They almost made Noah wish he'd spent his youth hanging out with the kids who liked breaking into cars, not the ones who enjoyed repairing them – those criminal skills would have been mighty handy now.

But schools, schools were best of all. Most folks underestimated schools. They'd only ever seen them as places for learning, but a homeschooled kid like Noah didn't have that disadvantage. He didn't see a lunchroom as a place for gossip and the dreary routine of half-warmed burgers, he saw it as a place where people worked to prepare food, vast amounts of food, much of it preserved for storage on an efficiently industrial scale. Then there were lockers. People abandoned all sorts of things in lockers. An old lighter might not amount to much, but go through a few hundred of those teenage hiding holes and you could end up with a heap of lost treats, from the odd bag of weed to a well oiled flick-knife. Staff rooms had coats and coffee, janitor's closets had tools, even corridors had vending machines.

School libraries he could take or leave. Paper made good kindling, but so did fallen leaves for half the year, and the stuff they'd used in the last generation of textbooks wasn't great for wiping your ass - too slick and shiny, not like the good old college books Ma had kept around the house. Not that he'd have ever dreamed of wiping his ass with Mama's books. Life wouldn't have been worth living the day he'd done a thing like that.

Still, wander around a school long enough and eventually you end up in the library. This one was well preserved despite the devastation that had descended on the rest of the town. The books were spotted with mildew and rats had made a nest in a corner full of what had once been stacks of magazines. The banks of computers along two walls stared at the world with dead, blank screens, like giant square eyes on a row of corpses. But there was still reading to be had.

As he strolled through the library something caught Noah's eye. The familiar spine of one of the books, bold gold letters against a blue background, one his father had had. Noah pulled it off the shelf. A sense of warm familiarity spread through him as he eased open the cover, revealing the packed pages behind a picture of a jet plane and a man with a gun. He flicked through, lost for a while in scenes he hadn't read in half a lifetime. Tales of fights and chases, the likes of which had thrilled him as a kid. But even better were the scenes in bars, casinos and shopping centers, reminders of the rich life that had once been. A world of comforts that seemed decadent now.

At last he sighed and stowed the book away in his bag for later. The sun was sinking in the sky and part of him knew he ought to move on. But where would he find better shelter tonight?

"C'mon, let's get more books," he said to Bourne. "See if

they've got your namesake. Don't reckon we'll have to worry about a library card."

He prowled down the rows of fiction, looking for stylish spines or familiar names. How long had he stood looking through that one book, lost to the world and everything in it? How great would it be to find more of the same, something comforting to see him through the next terrible winter? Not as great as a crate more of Paul's whiskey, sure, but good enough to make this whole school business worthwhile.

Behind him a door creaked open.

Noah spun around. A man stood in the entrance to the library. Dressed in body armor with metal plates protecting his arms and legs, his height added to his intimidating bulk. He raised a musket towards Noah, eyes sparkling above the red bandana around his neck.

Drawing Bourne as he moved, Noah turned towards the library's other exit, a pair of double doors leading onto a stairwell. But another man blocked it, also armed and armored with the same red bandana and the same bow and arrow symbol stenciled across his chest.

If there was one thing worse than men with weapons it was men with uniforms.

"Hold there, Dionite." The first guard's voice rang clear with a hint of a European accent. Between that and his cropped black hair he could have been the villain from one of those precious spy books.

Noah jerked to his left, out of sight between two rows of shelves. He ran down the aisle, only to see the second soldier appear at the far end.

The guy's gun wasn't raised yet, and there were only yards between them. Straight on looked better than turning back.

Noah kept running, slamming into the guard. The man

dropped his gun and grabbed for Noah. The two of them staggered back and forth, banging against shelves, books tumbling down around them.

Noah yanked his knee upward. The soldier was wearing a cup and pain jolted up Noah's leg, but he'd managed enough impact to hurt the other guy, who crumpled over wheezing on the floor.

Fast as he could, Noah disentangled himself and ran for the empty doorway.

Except that it wasn't empty. As he burst through the doors and into the top of the stairwell he almost ran straight into another soldier, a woman with long, black hair. Noah shifted his grip on Bourne, tried to hit the woman over the head with the pistol, but she was faster. She ducked under his swing and grabbed his arm, trying to drag it around behind him.

Noah yelped in pain and staggered back, trying to ram the woman against the wall. But the floor was smooth and the soles of his shoes were worn flat. He couldn't get the grip to gain an advantage, while she maneuvered around behind and then slid him forwards, slamming him up against the stair rail and twisting his arm further.

At last his numbed fingers gave in and Bourne slid from his grip, clattering to the ground. The woman kicked the pistol away and Bourne span out over the stairwell, tumbling towards the ground below.

"No!" Noah jerked back, the rail giving him enough leverage to bring his greater height into play. With the soldier off balance, he snaked his left arm around behind her shoulder, got a grip and pulled. She stumbled against his outstretched leg and lost her footing, tumbling down the stairs.

Not for the first time, Noah found himself grateful for the experience he'd gained fighting Jeb and Pete when they were young. A younger brother had to learn all the hardest, filthiest tricks if he was ever to stay standing.

He followed the soldier down the stairs, leaping over her as she started to rise, turning back for a kick that sent her sprawling once more. Better to fight dirty than to fight half-assed.

Glancing around on the landing below, he looked without luck for any sign of Bourne, then he hurried down the flight of stairs, pausing again as he reached the second floor.

There the pistol was, lying just in front of a classroom doorway. Noah ran over and bent down to scoop up his traveling companion.

A shadow slid out of the doorway and what felt like a meteor strike slammed against the side of Noah's head. He sank to his knees as spots danced across his vision. He tried to reach for Bourne but only fumbled uselessly as the world split in two and spun around him.

"Dionite scum."

Another blow, against the back of his head this time. Noah sprawled flat on his front, cold tiles pressing against his face. He turned his head just enough to see the first soldier looking down at him, pure disdain in his eyes. What the hell was this guy's problem? What was a Dionite? And who cared this much about a bunch of old books?

"Taking you back to Apollo," the soldier said, his accent giving the words a harsh edge.

Before Noah could even wonder who or what Apollo was, the soldier's musket butt descended one last time, smashing against Noah's face and sending him into darkness.

CHAPTER 5
A PLACE OF SAFETY

IN EVERY STORY Noah had ever read or watched, when the hero got knocked out he woke up in captivity, usually someplace dark—whether it was a prison cell, the bowels of a ship, the boot of a car, or a secret bunker buried somewhere in the mountains. Two things told Noah this wasn't one of those stories. First, he wasn't yet in that darkened room, waiting for some pissed off guy on a power trip with slicked back hair and a bad accent to interrogate him. And second, he was no kind of hero.

His first awareness was the feeling in his feet, a stuttering stab of pain as he was dragged along, toes trailing on the hard, broken surface of a poorly kept road. If there was one thing Noah's feet could recognize by touch, it was a poorly kept road.

Sight would have made it all easier, of course. He could have looked around, got his bearings, prepared himself for the weight of his own body tugging mercilessly at his shoulders as the soldiers dragged him along with his arms hauled around their necks. Might have been he could have started finding his feet sooner, getting them underneath him before that big damn pothole nearly smashed his big toe.

But no, sight didn't even come second, as he mustered

the will to drag his weary eyes open. Second was hearing, the sound of their footsteps on the road, of one soldier cursing under his breath in what sounded like Russian, and what Noah's befuddled brain took for the sound of a town up ahead, folks talking and walking and going about their day. A sound he hadn't heard in years, and hadn't expected to ever hear again.

Next came smell, the fearsome body odor of someone who'd spent far too long wrapped in layers of armor and needed cleaning up worse than a dog that had been rolling in shit. And then the taste of blood in Noah's own mouth, which was hardly surprising given the way his last memory went down.

So by the time he finally forced his eyes open and raised his head into the fading light of day, Noah had a pretty good idea of what was going on around him.

The town still came as a shock.

It was one thing to hear the sound of hundreds of people all in one place, voices bouncing off buildings, the rumble of cart wheels and the demands for someone to get out of the goddamn way. It was another thing altogether to see it and believe it. Noah blinked a few times before he really registered what was ahead of him.

The soldiers dragged him between deserted buildings, densely packed by the standards of this part of the world. They could have still been in the town where they had found him, or in another like it. Noah could only guess one way or the other. The one thing he was sure of was the street ahead was blocked by a wall at least a dozen feet high and built of all kinds of rubble. There were sections of battered bricks, probably pulled from the ruins of other houses and crudely mortared together. There were lumps of stone, some rough, some neatly cut and stacked. There were stretches of old iron work, overturned trucks with corrugated plates bolted across the gaps. It was the patchwork quilt of defensive positions, like something God's grandma might have made out of the scraps in the bottom of her sewing box.

It was the best built new thing Noah had seen since the sky started falling.

He dragged one foot forward and in the space of a few stumbling footsteps managed to get himself upright. The soldiers stepped back, the man shaking his head in amusement, the woman just scowling.

"Holy fucking Jesus on a scooter," Noah said, then thought of how his Ma would have responded to such language. That grandma thought had flung family into the forefront of his mind. "Pardon my language, but that there is impressive."

"Keep moving." The third soldier, the one who'd knocked Noah out, strode past them and gestured towards the gates being held open by two more impatient looking guards. They wore the same red bandanas and logo that was daubed across his captors' body armor, across the better patches of wall, even on a ragged red flag fluttering above the gate.

When Noah didn't respond, the woman gave him a shove with the butt of her musket, sent him stumbling on down the road.

"No need for that, sweetheart," Noah said. "Pretty smile like yours, all you had to do was- of."

The lead soldier wasn't much gentler than he'd been at the school, his fist hitting Noah's stomach with a force that spoke to anger and frustration or a really good workout.

"Respect the guard, Dionite," the soldier said, grabbing Noah by the collar and dragging him towards the gate.

In other circumstances, Noah might have fought back. The fellow was about the same height as him, and though his extra bulk looked to be all muscle, not everyone knew how to use their own strength. But there was the armor, the gun, the two other guards behind them and more up ahead. And self-preservation aside, Noah was intensely curious to see what lay behind those walls.

"Lieutenant Poulson." One of the guards on the gate saluted Noah's captor, and Poulson let go of Noah long enough to return the gesture. Then they were through, and those gates of plate steel were dragged back on what looked to be wheels taken from old cars. They clanged to a stop and bolts were thrown into place with a terrible finality that echoed down the street.

And what a street.

Every building was intact. Sure, some of them had seen repairs, like the hardware store with plyboard and plastic windows where its glass front had once been or the house down a side street with a canvas roof. But many of them looked untouched by the ravages of the past twenty years, and not one had been allowed to slip into neglect. The walls were clean, paintwork fresh, everything upright and in order. Little statues stood out front of many of the houses or stared from windows - some guy with goat's legs in one, a fat Buddha in another, a bearded man clutching a thunderbolt in a third. Religious icons, too - several crosses, squiggly script he didn't recognize, a couple of Stars of David. It seemed this was a praying sort of town.

The people matched the street's fine condition. Noah had met some folks in decent health in his travels. The odd hunter who'd kept himself in game dinners and furs for the winter, or couples who'd grabbed the right supplies to thrive in the wilderness. Even one or two farmers who'd managed to make their lands work right, though most were just scraping by. But a community or a decent sized caravan like the one he'd followed south? Those could never find enough food and medicine to really thrive, only hold themselves together and to keep each other going.

This place was different. These people weren't just well fed, or clear of the scars inevitable in a world without emergency rooms to hand. They were clean, their clothes neat and well patched. A prouder man might have felt ashamed to come among them in Noah's own ragged coat and sweat-stained shirt, but Noah was determined not to be that man. He straightened his shoulders, brushed the dried blood from his chin, held himself upright. Nobody made the Brennan boys feel like dirt, even when dirt was what they were wearing.

"Where to?" he asked.

The guard to his right laughed. He was mighty tolerant for a man Noah had tried to kick in the balls.

"To the prison," he said. Noah realized his was the Russian-sounding accent and that Lieutenant Poulson's was something more softly alien. What was with this place – had Virginia been invaded by the goddamn Europeans? Folks back home would have had things to say about that, and none of them friendly.

But as they marched him down the street, Noah heard familiar accents too, mostly local but some from deeper in the south or up the east coast. This place was thriving, and it still seemed to be American.

Something else grabbed his attention as they made their way towards an ugly concrete building on the far side of town. A girl, somewhere in her teens, scrawny as a spring fawn. She shadowed them as they walked, peering at Noah through gaps in the crowd, scurrying across junctions rather than staying out in the open. Her ragged clothes would have fit in anywhere else, but here they were distinct, and while the folks around them seemed determined to ignore her, to Noah she stood out.

They exchanged glances as he passed, her look filled as

much with curiosity as with a challenge to him, wanting to know what this disheveled stranger was about. Places like this had hot water, mirrors, and sharp razors. There weren't many beards here as wildly impressive as his, and even without the escort he'd have been distinctive.

"If I was you, I would not be looking so happy." Poulson glared at Noah. "Your friends are not going to save you."

"No change there then," Noah said. "I can count my friends on the fingers of one ass-cheek."

At last they came to a complex of grim concrete buildings, barbed wire trailing across the tops of the walls, dead cameras still standing on a couple of posts around the yard. The sign out front still held the words "County Jail," though the name of the county had been whited out and the word 'Apollo' neatly painted over the top.

Seemed these folks took pride in everything, even the dark places they reserved for crooks and strangers.

The raggedy girl stopped a hundred yards from the jail, hovered anxiously in an alley, her eyes flitting between Noah and the flat gray edifice. At the gate, a smaller door swung open on well-oiled hinges and Noah was shoved once more, this time across the doorstep and into an exercise yard. There wasn't much exercise going on, only two guards taking a break at a faded wooden table. Again there were religious icons all around the place – a cross in one corner of the yard, a bunch of little statues along railings and ledges. It was as if someone had taken a great big guide to world religions and shaken the pictures out all over this town and its jail. He wouldn't have been surprised if the Pope and the Dalai Lama had rounded the corner laughing about who was getting into heaven first.

Well, maybe a bit surprised. He'd heard only the faintest and least reliable of rumours about what was happening in the rest of the world, but if the Pope or the Dalai Lama were still alive so long after the apocalypse then he'd be pretty surprised. Like all the great musicians, all the top politicians, all the innovators, artists, actors, and damn near everyone else in the world, they were almost certainly dead. Just a handful of people were left, and some of them still insisted on locking him up.

It wasn't until another door clanged open and he was led into the prison building itself that Noah saw his fellow inmates. Suddenly the jail didn't seem such a bad idea. These were folks such as he'd met on the trail, only more so - rougher, angrier, hairier, more scarred. As he passed from a tiled corridor into a two story hallway lined with barred cells, a great noise of howling and whooping rose around them. Hands stretched out between the bars, clawing at the empty air. Savage looking men and women, all heavily tattooed, some with sharpened teeth or nails cut down to points. There was none of the neatness or cleanliness so prevalent in the town, but wild flowing hair, mohawks and dreadlocks, beards in a dozen different styles, and most of them dressed in little more than loincloths or a few scraps of fur.

"See what happens when you come for us?" Poulson paused in the middle of the hall and gestured towards Noah. "We get you all in the end."

Noah tried to protest, but his words were drowned out by the clamor of voices, all yelling at Poulson and the guards. Heavy hands dragged Noah down the last few yards of the hall and flung him into an empty cell. One more clang - the day's signature sound - and he was behind bars, just like his neighbor Mrs. Tallowitz had always predicted.

He doubted she would have pictured it happening like this.

The cell held only two pieces of furniture - a lidless toilet and a bed with a stained, threadbare mattress. But threadbare was still better than the no mattress Noah usually had. He sat down on it, leaning back against the wall, able to feel the wire mesh of the bed frame through the feeble padding.

The cell was maybe seven feet each way, enough space for a tall man to lie down but not much spare. Every inch of it gray except for a cross painted on the back wall - it looked like these folks liked to keep people holy but didn't trust them with the sort of crucifix you could take down and maybe stab someone with. Noah hadn't been stuck with walls so close around him for a good long time. It wasn't long before he could see them filling the edges of his vision, feel them closing in around him. His chest tightened like the jail was squeezing him in a vice grip.

He took a deep breath, focused on the open hallway beyond the bars, tried to keep his shit together.

"We've been through worse," he said, trying to convince himself. "Ain't that right buddy?"

He patted the empty holster where Bourne should have been, an absence that felt like a missing limb.

He reached up for his top left pocket, looking to steady his nerves with a smoke, but his cigarettes were gone. So was his lighter, his penknife, and as he frantically patted around his pockets he soon found everything else was too.

Sorrow turned to anger, then back to a terrible tension as he tilted his head and saw the walls closing in against him.

"Goddammit." His hand drifted back down to the empty holster. "I really am alone."

CHAPTER 6
BEAUTY AND A BEATING

Dawn was creeping through the bars of the cell when they came back for Noah, waking him from the little sleep he'd gotten despite the occasional howl from one of his fellow captives. Several of them seemed to suffer from nightmares, and he reckoned he would too if they kept him here long with the tightening walls and the yelling in the night. Someone had clearly been in pain, screaming every hour or so, and Noah was willing to bet the townsfolk didn't waste medicine on prisoners.

They provided food at least. There'd been some sort of slop before lights out, dished in plastic bowls so old and scratched they were probably no more hygienic than the poorly cleaned toilet in the corner of the cell. His stomach had been growling by then and he wolfed the lot down, only stopping at the end of licking the bowl to wonder if they'd put anything harmful in it. But why take him alive if that was their plan?

The bowl still sat by the bars of his cell when two soldiers marched in through the cold gray light and the silence that had finally fallen somewhere in the deep of night. Noah was waking up - the dawn would do that for you if you lived in the wild - and when they stopped by his cell he propped himself up on an elbow, watching them as casually as he could.

"Mornin' ladies." He rubbed his sleep crusted eyes, gave an exaggerated yawn. "I believe I ordered breakfast with my wake-up call?"

If these two thought he was funny, they didn't show it. It made Noah miss the Russian fellow from the day before. At least he knew how to laugh.

A heavy key turned in the lock and the cell swung open.

"Come with us," one of them said. "Sergeant Burns wants to see you."

"You didn't say the magic word," Noah said, sitting up and stretching his arms.

The guard reached him in two swift strides, slammed a metal club into his side.

Noah crumpled over as pain blazed through him.

"That magic enough for you?" she said.

He eased himself to his feet, wincing as he moved. Had that click been a rib cracking?

"After you," he said through gritted teeth.

"Oh no, wise-ass. After you."

The room they took him to looked like it had a long history of interrogations. Shattered remnants around the edges of the hole showed where observers had once watched conversations through one-way glass, and the animosity unleashed against that window had clearly extended to a hatred of the space itself. The table bolted down in the center of the room was charred and a little warped in one leg. It took a certain retarded determination to try to set fire to a metal table, and Noah almost admired whichever prisoner had tried it.

Then there was the mural on the wall, a stylishly rendered lightning bolt crossing over an ankh. He'd have admired it a lot more if it didn't seem like another part of this place's craze for religion.

No-one cuffed him or clapped him in irons. He was kind of disappointed to find that they didn't even consider him worth tying up, though relief outweighed that by a fair amount. Where there were free hands there was hope, as his Grandpa had never said.

They pressed him into a plastic chair and left him alone, taking long enough when closing the door that he could see the guards lurking outside, all with metal beating sticks at their sides, one with a musket.

"This is what I expected to wake up in," he said to the world in general. "Dim light through a barred window, distant dripping noises, maybe a rat or two just out of sight."

"You expected to wake up?" A woman's voice emerged from the room beyond the broken mirror. Noah squinted to make out her shape in the shadows, an indistinct patch amid a larger darkness.

"I don't have high standards," he said, "but that's one of them, sure."

"I wouldn't be getting any expectations if I were you." She moved suddenly forward, vaulted through the broken window and landed surely on her feet. But even though the sudden movement made Noah jump, it sure wasn't the most striking thing about her.

Whoever else this Sergeant Burns was, she was the most beautiful woman Noah had seen in the best part of a decade. Her eyes were the green of a forest on a fine spring morning, and Noah knew he was in trouble when he started thinking poetically. But how could he help it? She had wavy auburn hair tied back to reveal tattoos that ran from her neck across her shoulders and down her arms. Her tank top could have been chosen to show off her figure, but more likely was meant to show off her ink, which appeared again from beneath cut-off shorts and ran down her legs. The woman would have been a work of art in her own right, but with intricate swirls and pinpoint pictures adorning her skin she became art laid upon art, a moment of breath-taking wonder in this place of pain and confinement.

Her club crashed down on the table, denting the top. Noah jumped again.

"Got enough of an eyeful?" she growled. "Or should I take off my shirt and show you the rest?"

"If you're offering…" Even knowing what would follow, Noah couldn't resist.

Sure enough, the club slammed into his shoulder, almost knocking him from his seat. He clutched his shoulder, the movement only adding to his pain. Why did folks do that, he wondered. Did they think their hands would somehow gain magical healing powers, make it all better at the touch of flesh? He sure as hell wasn't feeling any magic.

Burns prowled around the edge of the room, circling in and out of his vision.

"What were you doing at the school?" she asked, stopping to lean across the table towards him. "What information were you after?"

"No information," Noah replied. "Just supplies. I was hoping to find food."

"In a library?" Burns snorted. "Yeah right."

She started prowling again, slapping the club against the palm of her hand, a steady drum beat of menace.

"What's the plan?" she asked. "Go through the old sewers maybe? Because I'll tell you now, we scooped up the municipal plans years ago. You and the rest of the savages won't get anywhere that way."

"No plan," Noah replied. "No savages. I'm just a drifter looking for supplies. Check my pack. Would a savage be carrying a book, or a set of snares, or, umm-"

"Or this?" She reached round into a holster at the back of her belt and pulled out Bourne.

Relief swept through Noah like a good-natured flood. Bourne wasn't lost. He still had something to cling onto in the wilds.

Well, he might if they somehow agreed to give the gun back.

And if they agreed to let him go.

Damn, there were a lot of ifs today. So much for his rising spirits.

"So you're just some innocent drifter." Burns turned Bourne as if inspecting the barrel for clues. "Some innocent drifter who goes sneaking around towns, and who pulls a gun at the first sight of the Apollonian Guard."

"It ain't a good idea to roam the wilds unarmed," Noah said. "There's a lot of bad people out there."

"There certainly are." Burns glared pointedly at him.

"I'm not bad people," Noah said. "Whoever you think I am, I ain't. I don't know no plans or no maps, or no Dionites, whatever the hell one of them is."

"I didn't say anything about Dionites." Molly stuck Bourne back through her belt. She looked triumphant.

"Your friends, they said it." Noah straightened in his seat. He had to focus, had to be real clear so he didn't dig himself no further into trouble. But her leaning forward like she kept doing wasn't helping matters none. "That Poulson fellow, he called me Dionite, or Diorite, or Dynamite, or some such shit."

"Oh, so now you're pretending like you don't even know what I'm talking about?"

"I don't! I swear to God or Bourne there, or those mighty

fine tattoos, I swear I don't-"

She lashed out with the club again. He tried to jerk back, was too slow, wound up sprawling on the floor, the back of his head pounding where it hit the concrete, cheek hot and sticky with his own blood.

She stood over him, the club pressed against his throat.

"I can do all kinds of things to you here," she said. "Not just beatings, though I'm more than happy to lay that down all over your sorry, savage ass. We have pliers back there in the other room. Knives too. And I've got quite an imagination when I get riled. You'd be amazed the places I've found to cut at, to squeeze, to rip. I've got a little blowtorch, one of those old gas ones. Of course, getting gas is hard these days, but it's worth spending it when I think we're in danger. When I think some Dionite's tongue needs loosening."

She reached around behind her back again, pulled a pair of wires from her belt. There were clamps on the ends.

"See these?" She dangled the clamps down in Noah's face. "Electric cables, like people used to use to jump start cars. Of course, I was too young to ever do that. The only use I get from them is clamping them onto some asshole who thinks he's too big and too clever to talk. Then I get the battery we keep for these special occasions, and I attach it to the other ends of these wires. And then that savage asshole, he gets to see how electricity works for the first time in twenty years.

"So, what have you got to say to me and my cables?"

"You're rusty," Noah replied.

"What?"

"I'm talking to your cables, like you asked. And the clamps, they're all rusted up. No way you've ever latched them onto anyone. I'm starting to wonder if maybe you've got a gentler touch than you're making out."

He'd expected her to get angry, to shout at him some

more. But instead she seemed to seize up into a terrible rigid silence, her face frozen but something glittering like a razor blade deep in her eyes.

Then the club came down again and again and again, battering him as he curled up around himself, arms defending his head and chest. The blows came so thick and fast that the world merged into a haze of pain, and when he finally emerged she was leaning back against the desk, panting, looking just as stunned as he felt.

"I..." She said. "I'm..."

Her expression hardened again.

"We don't need electric leads to make your life tough," she said. "You think you're so smart, but I don't even need to lift a finger to make you squirm. And don't think I won't, when Apollo's safety's at stake.

"Vostok!"

The door opened and the Russian-sounding fellow stepped inside. He gave an exaggerated wince as he looked at Noah, brow furrowing beneath his shock of blond hair.

"Sergeant Burns?" he asked.

"Take this wretch back to the cells," she said. "But I hear that they're getting crowded now, so we'll have to throw him in with someone else. Make him bunkmates with Blood Dog, let him make some new friends."

"But we've still got–"

"No," Burns said. "In with Blood Dog. Am I clear?"

Vostok hung his head, walked over and dragged Noah to his feet.

"Come on, my friend," he said. "Let's get you settled."

As they left the room Noah took one last look back. Though his vision was blurred by the swelling bruise around one eye, he got a last good look at Burns leaning over the desk, ponytail hanging down past her face, her whole body sagging as she took long, deep breaths. Hot as she was, brutal as she was, he felt a strange stab of pity for the stunned looking young woman.

Hearing the howls coming from the cells, Noah doubted that feeling of pity would last.

CHAPTER 7
MAKING FRIENDS

The cells were almost silent, the prisoners taken out for who knew what reason. Noah figured they weren't all getting the kind of treatment he'd had from Sergeant Burns – that would run the guards ragged, even the ones who got a kick out of beating on folks.

He didn't think Burns was that kind. Or maybe he just hoped she wasn't. Shame to have an ugly soul behind such a pretty face.

His new cell was in the corner of the same block as the one he'd spent the night in, but on the second floor, opening onto a walkway that ran around the perimeter of the hall. Looking out through the barred door, a row of cells lay ahead and to his right, the echoing space of the prison to his left. Like his previous cell, it had concrete walls and a filthy john in one corner, but unlike that cell it had a pair of bunks instead of one bed.

The cell fell like dread across Noah's mind. Any other time his heart would have been racing, but it was only just slowing down after the fight-or-flight-or-lie-here-getting-beaten moment with Sergeant Burns. It wasn't that the cell seemed better by comparison, it was just that he had no reserves left to panic with.

Burns had no way of knowing how he felt about enclosed

spaces, but if she had she could hardly have planned this better. The corner cell let in even less light than his previous abode, and with only part of one wall not consumed with flat concrete there wasn't much sign of space or open air. Even if he pressed his face against the bars, he'd still have a wall looming at him from the right, albeit one lined with cells instead of that crushingly flat gray.

Though no-one was around the upper bunk clearly belonged to someone – the sheets were dishevelled and there was a tally of scratches on the wall above, like someone had learned about prisons in an old movie and wanted to make sure he was living the authentic 1940s experience. You couldn't tell much about a fellow from his stained bed sheets and a bunch of scratches, but they didn't make Blood Dog seem any more appealing than his name already had.

Noah shifted an old magazine and lay back gratefully on the bottom bunk. He'd tried not to show it as Vostok led him back to the cell, but his head was spinning a little from the beating, and every inch of his body contributed to a single massive ache. He wanted to work out what was going on with this place, to piece together a plan to convince them he wasn't one of these Dionites so they would let him out. But he was too damn tired and in too much pain to deal with any of it.

He closed his eyes, shutting out the closeness of the bunk above him, the walls looming in from every direction, the terrible itch of panic being swallowed by exhaustion in the back of his brain, and let his mind wander off into sleep.

When he woke, it was getting dark again. He'd have to be careful not to let this turn into a habit. Night was for sleeping, in prison or anywhere else, and the last thing his exhausted body needed was a screwed up sleep pattern.

There was noise in the prison hall now, the clatter of footsteps and chatter of voices as dozens of men were returned to their cells. He could hear the rattling of keys in locks and the repeated jangle of chains, but none of the wild howling that had greeted him on his arrival. Maybe that had been a show for the guards, or a way to intimidate the new prisoner, or just a strange mood that seized these folks at night. Maybe it would be back as soon as he tried to sleep. Whatever it had been, it wasn't part of this routine.

Footsteps came closer and a guard appeared, unlocked Noah's cell and then took a step back. He looked wary despite his body armor and the club on his belt. When Noah saw the prisoner being escorted, he understood why.

Blood Dog. Noah assumed it was him because he was being ushered into the cell, and because of the big red Doberman tattooed on one cheek. He was a ridiculous and terrifying example of humanity. Vostok, the guard, was a big guy with a good couple of inches on Noah and muscles to match, but this guy would have loomed over even him. Like Sergeant Burns, he was covered in tattoos and wore a tank top to show them off, but there the similarity ended. Blood Dog must have weighed twice as much as Burns, being built like a wrestler who'd eaten fifteen cows and then hit the gym non-stop for a year. His scowl was infinitely more convincing than hers, plastered across a face that didn't so much sit on top of his body as protrude out of it, a solid mass of muscle with little distinction between head, neck and the upward sweep of his shoulders.

"What the fuck you looking at?" he growled as he stepped into the cell.

A dozen answers leaped unbiddenly into Noah's mind. Many of them clever, but it wouldn't have been smart to utter them out loud.

"Nothing," he mumbled.

"What you doing with my bikes?" Blood Dog crossed the cell to loom over Noah, even as the key rattled again in the door of the cell, locking them in together.

"Your bikes?" Noah looked around in confusion. What in high hell was this guy talking about?

"My bikes." A finger fat as salami pointed at the old magazine Noah had discarded to get into bed. Now that he paid more attention, he saw that its once glossy pages were covered with pictures of bikes, some of them tearing down highways under men in leather jackets and neatly kept beards, others sitting in studio imitations of workshops underneath young women with less facial hair and a lot less clothes.

"Sorry." Noah rolled out of his bunk and bent down to scoop up the magazine. As he moved his tired and battered muscles screamed in protest, stiffening up so that instead of bending down into a neat crouch he sprawled on the concrete, landings on top of Blood Dog's magazine and further crumpling the already old and fragile pages.

"You think you're funny?" Blood dog growled, in a tone that made it clear what he thought of funny people, and that it was a thought funny people would regret. "You some kind of wise guy?"

A booted foot nudged hard at Noah's arm, making him wince as it knocked against his bruises. The intensity of Blood Dog's presence filled the space of the already enclosed cell, closing him into an ever smaller fraction of the room. A room whose concrete floor now filled most of his vision, the wall occupying the rest only inches from his face, the door closed and locked and not to open until who knows when. It was all way too much. His heart was pounding like it might burst any moment, the whole space drawing in closer and closer and closer.

He closed his eyes, took a series of deep breaths.

"What you doing now wise guy?" Blood Dog nudged him harder with his foot. Noah winced. "Working up some more funny, huh?"

"No funny," Noah managed to say.

He pushed himself up onto all fours, then onto his knees. Then he opened his eyes and picked up the magazine, held it up towards Blood Dog.

"I'm real sorry," he said. "We've clearly got off to a bad start here. My name's Noah, they've put me in here to-"

"My bikes." Blood Dog snatched the magazine, stepped back so he could look at it in a better light. Noah took the opportunity to hurriedly get to his feet.

"Sorry about that," he said. "I didn't know they were your bikes. If I had, I'd obviously have shown them more respect, on account of how they're mighty fine bikes and you're... Well, you're you."

Blood Dog scowled again.

"What's that mean?" he said. "What have you heard?"

"Nothing." Noah backed up against the bunks as Blood Dog once again towered over him. This close he could see the tattoos in more detail despite the poor light in the cell. There was the red dog emblazoned across one cheek and an Italian flag on the other. The word 'HATE' in gothic letters down one side of his neck, and an automatic pistol on the opposite side, a trail of empty shell casings cascading from it down onto his shoulder and what looked like it might be the start of a dead body sprawled across his chest. And though Noah couldn't make them out with their owner glaring down at him, it was clear that the tattoos carried on across the top of Blood Dog's head.

What kind of lunatic got a tattoo of a dead body? And not a good tattoo either, from what Noah could see.

"Let me tell you what you haven't heard." Blood Dog was so close that the stink of decay and old cigarettes washed across Noah on the thug's hot breath. "I ain't from around here. I'm from up where they make proper gangsters, see? And down here, around you faggoty-ass rednecks, that makes me the boss, the fucking don of all you raggedy little douchebags who think you count as gangsters. That's made me the boss since I got to this piss-hole town, and it'll make me boss again once this trial shit is done and they let me out of here. You understand, wise guy?"

"Absolutely, yes."

"Yes who?"

"Yes, boss?"

"Good little redneck."

Was this guy for real? Noah felt like he was facing some cartoon of a Mafiosi thug, or some weird exaggerated vision brought on by exhaustion and muddled memories of gangster films.

Then Blood Dog's fist hit him in the gut, and as he puked up what little there was in his stomach he knew the guy was for real.

"Top bunk's my bunk." Blood Dog stepped back to avoid the vomit. He looked like he might be about to laugh. "Bottom bunk's for my bikes." He took the magazine, laid it carefully in the center of the bottom mattress, smoothing down the cover like he was straightening the sheets over a sleeping child. Noah hoped like hell that this guy had never been near a real child. "You can sleep there too, long as you don't disturb my bikes." Blood Dog turned back to glare at him. "Understand?"

Noah nodded, wiped a trail of puke from the side of his mouth. "Got it."

"Good." Blood Dog patted Noah's cheek, then turned and swung himself up onto the top bunk. The whole frame creaked beneath him and among all the pain and the acidic taste of bile in his mouth another thought occurred to Noah – the bottom bunk might not be such a great space to sleep anyway. Could any bed frame hold up under the weight of Blood Dog? And if it gave in, what would happen to the guy underneath?

"What's your name, wise guy?" Blood Dog asked, lying back with his hands beneath his head.

"Noah."

"That's a pussy name. I don't like it. I'm gonna call you Pukey. You OK with that Pukey?"

"Yes," Noah said. It wasn't like he could stop this guy calling him whatever he wanted. He'd take the name Pixie Rainbow if it saved him from more beatings.

"Yes who?" Blood Dog growled.

"Yes, boss."

"Good boy, Pukey."

Noah sank down against the wall, staring out through the bars at what passed for open space in the hallway beyond.

This was why he hated people.

CHAPTER 8
LIVING IN HOPE

BLOOD DOG WAS A SNORER. And not just any snorer, but the kind of colossal, echoing snorer whose night time sounds shook the very walls of the cell. Noah wouldn't have said it was the worst noise he'd heard all week - after all, there had been the thud of Burns's club against his body, the clang of endless gates slamming shut behind him, and of course the noises Blood Dog made when he was actually awake. But any other week, maybe any other day, it would have been considered Noah's worst noise.

He opened his eyes, then remembered why he had kept them closed. This cell might never get properly lit, but it somehow never got properly dark either. With his eyes open he could see the mattress above bulging under the weight of his cell mate, threatening to bust through the wire mesh that held him in place and crush Noah beneath three hundred pounds of writhing muscles and crude tattoos. To his right, the wall pressed in against him both visually and physically. He hadn't dared move Blood Dog's magazine for fear that the muscle mountain would wake up first and start the day by beating anyone who'd touched his precious bikes. That left Noah with half a mattress to sleep on, and the bigger half left him pressed up against the wall, which made him twitchy as all hell, but was better than risking rolling out of bed into a pile of his own puke.

Sleep was hard enough to find with all that was going on in his own room, but to top it all off the next cell held a screamer.

It hadn't taken long, now that he had a second night to assess his surroundings, to work out that the pained screaming he'd heard came from more than one inmate. There was still the background shouting, the confused, incoherent yells of men and women waking from nightmares. Noah figured he'd be one of them soon enough the way things were going. But cutting through that was another sort of scream, the sort that came from real, coherent pain.

Some of it was arguments, prisoners yelling back and forth at each other, continuing fights that the guards had broken up during the day. That died down within an hour of lights out, an inability to reach each other preventing the arguments from ever reaching any climax, leaving the contenders to trail off into disappointed silence.

Then there were the repeated noises, the ones that started with a panicked yelp or a plea for mercy before descending into rhythmic grunting and muffled cries. Those sounds filled Noah with a terrible, gut-gripping horror for what his future held. But there was a sense of shame as well, as he remembered Mary the wheelbarrow lady from Tyrone's caravan and her own cries following him through the forest as Half-Skull did his dirty work. Could Noah have done something to save her? Probably not. Would anyone step in to help him if he fell victim to the same hideous crime here? Again, probably not.

But for all of the deep torment caused by those muffled sounds; for all of the dreadful grunting noises Blood Dog made in his sleep, like two pigs getting down with a baboon; for all of the nightmares that left people screaming and mumbling somewhere in the darkness; for all of that, the most immediate and pressing noise keeping Noah awake came from the next cell over. Because that noise, more than any of the others, that noise was persistent.

Whoever was in the next cell clearly had a lot on his mind. As the rest of the cells fell quiet, he was still muttering away to himself, his voice sometimes rising until another prisoner yelled at him to shut up. Which was how Noah learned that the mutterer's name was Iver, the way that other prisoners spat his name at him like a curse.

Iver's muttering might almost have been soothing if it had stayed nice and low like a bedtime story or the babbling of a brook; it could have eased Noah down into sleep. But, of course, it didn't stay quiet. That would have been too easy. Once the rest of the inmates were asleep, with no-one but Noah left to hear or protest at the sound, Iver's voice rose and fell - sometimes steady for long stretches as he jabbered to himself, sometimes jerking up and down from one word to the next. It was like listening to a broken radio as the dial was turned from station to station, unable to keep ahold of a channel, the subject skipping from fragments of songs and poetry to chanted nonsense to rambling discourses on medicine and books.

If he was this confused and distressed to listen to, Noah dreaded to think what it was like to be inside Iver's head. No wonder the guy couldn't sleep, with all this shit tumbling helter-skelter through his brain, not leaving him any rest behind the darkness of his eyes. With the walls pressing in on his own jittery mind, Noah could understand that kind of distress, could understand how it might chase away any hope of sleep.

And without sleep to help him through the night, Noah figured he might as well try to get some space. He rose from his bed, carefully avoiding crumpling the precious magazine, and winced as a creak of the wire frame disturbed Blood Dog. The criminal's snores fell silent for a moment and Noah clenched in fear of another confrontation. Then Blood Dog shifted, rolled onto his side, and started to snore again, the noise even more choked and bestial than before. No human soul should make a sound like that, but based on everything else he'd seen, Noah really wasn't sure Blood Dog had a soul. Hell, he might not even be human.

The moment of danger having passed, Noah rose to his feet, careful not to stand in the spot where he'd puked. It didn't seem likely the guards would clear that up. He wondered if they'd even give him the tools to do it himself, or if they left their prisoners to wallow in filth. Burns had said that she had ways to make him cooperate.

He closed his eyes and pictured Burns - her tight, curvy body, those tattoos running like a half made promise downward toward what was hidden beneath her clothes. If he could maybe work out what she wanted to hear, maybe avoid another beating, yet somehow find a way to keep the interrogations coming, then maybe, just maybe, he might actually enjoy being in here.

Blood Dog gave a strangled grunt, rolled over again, and settled into a more rhythmic snoring. Maybe 'enjoy' wouldn't ever be a part of this picture.

Noah took the two steps over to the iron bars that formed the door of his cell. If he pressed himself up against them and shifted his face so that the bars weren't in his eye line, then he could almost believe he was in the hall, that there was space and air and a high ceiling with a sky beyond. A breeze brushed his skin, the part of it not pressed up against the cold metal, and he breathed a sigh of relief.

Up close like this he could hear Iver more clearly, rambling away to himself only a half dozen feet and two steel doors to the right. A few of them seemed to be pleas for rescue, a repeated refrain rising like a guitar riff through the wilder sounds of an old rock song. Over and over the same phrase bubbled through the bass beat of murmured curses and the screeching solos of his ranting screams:

"They've got to come for me."

"They've got to come for me."

"They've got to come for me."

And then Noah heard it, the one word guaranteed to get his attention tonight, to hook him in and draw him closer to anybody's thoughts on any subject.

"Dionite."

Iver was talking quietly now. Noah tried to lean forwards, to move his ear closer for a better listen, but once you were pressed up against the bars of a cell there really was no further to go. He would need a different approach.

"Hey!" he hissed, trying for the delicate balance between loud enough for Iver to hear him and quiet enough to leave Blood Dog sleeping. "Hey, Iver!"

"Hey what hey who hey you hey Jude." Iver appeared at the bars of his cell. Noah caught a glimpse of pale dreadlocks against paler skin, of intricate tattoos and shapeless rags like so many of the prisoners were draped in. Bright eyes twitched back and forth, catching the light coming in through the windows in the ceiling, as wild and bewildered as Iver's words.

"Hey man," Noah whispered. "Over here."

Iver looked over towards him, his gaze filled with hope.

"Did they send you?" he asked. "Have you come to rescue me?"

"Who's they Iver?" Noah asked. "Is it the Dionites? Are you a Dionite?"

If he could find out more about these people maybe he could give Burns what she wanted, or at least persuade her of his uselessness as a source. After the pounding he'd taken earlier, he felt very motivated to make that happen.

Iver's brow furrowed in suspicion.

"I don't know," he said. "Do I know you? I don't think I know you, and I know lots of things. Wild things and wonderful things, body things and brain things. Do you know how to stitch up a hole in a broken heart? I did that once. Oh yes, I did. I was sure and steady, Coltrane smooth, Miles inspired, and I strung that poor muscle back together and it beat like the music like do-wop-de-do and he lived. Or maybe he didn't.

"Did you live? Or are you another ghost, another Moon ghost come to haunt our purgatory?"

"I'm not a ghost, Iver. Just a wanderer looking to get himself settled in some."

"Are you Walt Whitman? You have Walt Whitman hair and a Walt Whitman beard, but darker, like shadows. A negative of Walt Whitman. A scan on the wall. An x-ray that's never penetrated, not got through flesh to bone, not broken the innards open like they want to break me open. But they won't. None of you will. You'll see! You'll all see! They're coming for me!"

"Shh!" Noah glanced over his shoulder in panic as Iver's voice rose, but Blood Dog still looked and sounded to be asleep. "It's OK, it's OK, I'm not with them. Look, they've locked me up too, right?"

Iver nodded, smiled.

"That, sir, is logic," he declared loudly, then clamped a hand over his mouth. He lowered his voice to a whisper. "They don't like it when I talk. Back in the tribe they like it when I talk, they let me talk all I want about whatever I want, but not in here. Here they hate the wild ways and the wild people and freedom.

"I used to hate the wild ways, the parent ways, the ragged loose-living ways, but I was wrong. This is what happens when you turn your back on tradition." He pointed up towards the night sky, the debris belt even blurrier through the filthy glass ceiling. "Real tradition. Pre-civilization tradition, that flows like Mingus and sings like Simone. Tradition that's ways not rules, know what I'm saying?"

"Yeah, sure." Noah hadn't a clue, but saying that wouldn't get him what he wanted. "So you live in the wilds, huh? Is that where the Dionites live too?"

Iver stretched up on tiptoes, peered down at the floor of the prison hall.

"They've got to come for me," he said again, his voice small and trembling as a lost child. "Why aren't they here yet? They've got to come for me."

He leaned back, shook the bars of his cell.

"They've got to come for me!" he yelled into the darkness, his voice rising from a sob into a scream. "They've got to come for me!"

"Shut the fuck up, Iver!" someone bellowed from a nearby cell.

Iver shrank back, away from the bars and into the hidden recesses of his cell.

"Iver?" Noah said quietly. "It's OK Iver. We can still talk, just you and me, quiet like."

There was no response.

"Iver?" he said again. "You still there, Iver?"

But Iver had finally fallen silent, not even the quietest of crazed ramblings emerging from his mouth. Grateful as his other neighbors might have been, Noah found himself bitterly disappointed, seeing a chance to shape his situation snatched away.

He settled back down on his mattress, wincing once as his bruised flesh pressed against the sharp edge of the bedframe, and again as he unthinkingly rolled onto Blood Dog's precious magazine and felt it crumple beneath him.

He'd just have to hope it was battered enough already that Blood Dog couldn't tell the difference.

He closed his eyes, blocking out the mattress above and the wall to his side. Wishing there was some way to block out Blood Dog's snoring, Noah tried one more time to get to sleep.

CHAPTER 9
CHAIN GANG

If Noah had questions about why these folks went to the trouble of keeping prisoners – and given the state of the world beyond their wall he sure did – then those questions were quickly answered. And once he knew he could have kicked himself for not working it out.

The prisoners were there to work.

On his second morning in the cells he was woken by the sound of a guard rattling her club against the bars. This was followed by a slow march down to the main floor of the prison hall and through to what turned out to be a canteen. Amid the smells of unwashed bodies and of wood smoke from the stoves in the kitchen they were all marched in single file past a man with a ladle and a huge vat of porridge, who doled out gray-brown sludge into plastic bowls and handed one to each prisoner. Blood Dog got an extra full bowl and an obsequious smile from the server. Iver didn't even get eye contact. Noah received an inquisitive gaze, though he'd no clue whether that was down to the sight of a new face or the bruises with which he was so thoroughly decorated.

A woman came in before he had a chance to start eating, dressed in a red robe with a blue sash around the waist. A chain hung heavily around her neck decorated with three different crosses and an array of runes. When she entered, the dining hall fell silent, guards and prisoners alike came to a standstill. Spoons were left lying in bowls, batons hanging idle.

"This morning's prayer was crafted by Elder Khatri," the woman said. "Please bow your heads."

"Fuck you!" screamed one of the wilder men in the serving queue. "I ain't bowing for your gods or your shitty-"

He was cut short by a guard's club thudding into his stomach. He doubled over, his tray clattering to the floor. Another guard stepped up and they dragged him away.

"As I was saying," the robed woman continued, "today's prayer was crafted by Elder Khatri, and is entitled 'The Path We Will Walk'." She cleared her throat, unrolled a sheet of paper and then read. "Oh gods, who shaped Heaven and Earth, who gave humankind guidance when we were young, and who waited patiently through our long years of ignorance. The path we have walked in the past was a lost one, away from you, from your wisdom, from the lives you laid out for us. The path we walk now is one of finding ourselves, finding what we mean to you and you to us, finding the truth and the potential within ourselves, as human beings and as a people brought together in your light. The path we will walk, the path of the future, is dark to us now, but by your guidance it will be illuminated and by our obedience it will be found. We thank you for your warning, we thank you for your patience, we thank you for your guidance and we thank you for the path we will walk." She lifted her head and looked around the room. "Praise be to the gods."

"Praise be to the gods," the prisoners repeated with varying degrees of sincerity.

Noah shook his head and got back to his food. This place was messed up.

Breakfast, it turned out, was as much for distraction as for sustenance. While the prisoners were busy eating, guards walked down the lines of benches where they sat, counting off groups of half a dozen men and shackling them together with manacles and chains. Metal closed around Noah's left ankle, an area mercifully free of bruises, tying him to the next man over. He'd ended up at the end of a group, and while that meant he wouldn't have the opportunity to talk with Iver in the next gang over, it also saved him from a whole day in Blood Dog's company. The night had been more than enough.

The good thing about being put to work was that it got him into the open air. Noah's detail marched out through the prison yard and down a street to the town walls. He got another look at the town as he went. It was all so civilized. There were folks out picking up litter, others mending and painting a house in need of repair, and on one corner an old lady was reading stories to a group of little kids, getting them to count along with her and make the right animal noises. Emerging from the bleak brutality of the prison into the town created a sense of relief, but a sense of surreality too. Could these things really exist in the same space? Maybe not for long, because the prisoners were ushered swiftly past it all and out through a smaller gate than the one by which Noah had first arrived.

They were one of three chain gangs led out under the watchful eyes of half a dozen guards, Burns and Vostok among them. That at least was something working his way - a halfway friendly face and a pretty one among his overseers for the day. He was tempted to give Burns a wink, but she wasn't looking his way, too busy surveying the surrounding area, looking for threats or perhaps more innocent wanderers she could lock up and beat for information.

She looked more confident out here in body armor with

a chain gang than she had in the interrogation room. More relaxed and comfortable in herself, chatting with the other guards, even laughing, though she cut that short any time she approached the prisoners.

They were led to a group of ruined buildings in sight of the town walls, across an open expanse that might once have been houses. There Noah's group and one other were given picks and shovels to clear away the debris while a third team were put in charge of wheeling it away in barrows - large chunks to be used for construction, smaller debris to fill potholes in the nearby road.

The work itself was exactly as much fun as it looked, which was to say none at all. Noah thought himself to be in pretty good shape - hell, he'd had to be to live through the shit he'd seen - but hard labor was still hard labor, and the last few days had left his body less than helpful. He swung his pick, breaking up an old brick wall bit by bit. It was slow, aching work and, even more than the labor he resented the ever-present guards watching them from a dozen yards back, muskets ready in case anyone made a run for it.

But after one day and two nights in the cells, the mere experience of being back outdoors lifted Noah's spirits. The sun warmed his body and fresh air filled his lungs. He found himself humming a little tune as he chipped away at the brickwork, getting into a rhythm that helped him ignore his pain and just go with the simplicity of his body in action. Sure, he'd rather be walking the woods, checking his snares and looking for the next town to search, but he'd rather anything than being locked up in the terrible confines of the cells.

"What are you looking so chirpy about?"

Noah turned to see Burns standing off to his right, musket held loosely across her front, frowning at him for all she was worth.

"Why sergeant," Noah said, "I was just enjoying this fine weather we're having and the sight of those hills over yonder. But now I get the pleasure of your company too - could life get any sweeter?"

"What the hell's your problem, Brennan?" she asked, taking a step closer. "You don't strike me as mentally ill, and you've got enough sense to have lasted this long. So what keeps you from acting like a sane human being?"

"Apart from the beautiful woman who'd rather beat me than stop for a nice conversation?" Noah swung his pick, felt fragments of masonry bounce off his legs. "I'd say my problem was being ambushed by folks with guns, beaten senseless, and then locked up for the night with a man whose idea of fun probably involves feeding fluffy bunnies to gators."

"You chose your life, Brennan," she replied. "You can choose something different. Cooperate with me, tell me what I want to know. Not every cell holds a Blood Dog. Not every day includes a beating. Not every work detail means busting your ass beneath the blazing sun."

Noah paused, set the head of his pick on the ground and leaned on the handle. With a free hand he wiped the sweat from his brow.

"I've kind of got a liking for the blazing sun," he said. "Least the sun ain't got busted halfway across the heavens like the moon. Look up during the day and you'd never know the whole world had gone to hell, not unless you were all about fixing that world. Is that what you Apollo folks are about, rebuilding civilization one rubble heap at a time? Cause you'll sure be busy for a good few years yet."

"I'm the one asking the questions," Burns said. "Like what was your plan? What were you hoping to find once you got into town?"

"Look, two days ago I didn't even know that your

precious town existed. I was just mindin' my own business, lookin' for supplies. I stumble across some busted up place in the ass end of nowhere, up here in the hills, and I think to myself "hey, maybe there's some supplies left lying around'. So I go exploring. Only next thing I know your Lieutenant Poulson's pulling a gun on me, your man Vostok's beating me around the place, some other woman's throwing me down a stairwell, and not in a good sort of way. You want me gone, I'll go. But I don't know nothing about whatever it is you think I know about."

"Ignorance is the one thing I can believe of you. But that it's a coincidence you showed up just when the Dionites have been launching raids to try to get to the Oracle? I don't think so."

"The Oracle?"

"Don't make me laugh. You know full well what you were after, but if you think I'll talk about it, that I'll risk letting slip some detail you don't already know, then you're a bigger fool than you take me for."

"Don't suppose you've got a thing for fools?' Noah said. 'Cause I tell you, I've found some mighty romantic spots on the trail, and I get mighty loose lipped after I've gotten laid."

"Shut the hell up." She stamped right up to him, glared into his face. "Take up your pick and get back to work."

"Yes sir, sergeant, sir." It felt good to hit a nerve, to have even a fragment of control over his situation. Noah hefted his pickaxe and settled back into his rhythm.

The work stopped a couple of times for water, and each time Noah was surprised to realize how long had passed. Then came a break for lunch - hard bread and more water - and for each group in turn to be led around a corner so that they could all go for a piss. When they came back from that and started work again Noah once more found himself under Burns" watchful gaze.

"You got a first name, Sergeant Burns?" he asked after a while.

"Not one I'm going to tell you," she replied.

"But you know mine, it don't hardly seem fair."

"I've got to waste my day watching some stubborn Dionite knock down a wall and lie to me. Life is seldom fair."

"I'm trying to cooperate, really I am. I mean don't get me wrong, I ain't sayin' I ain't stubborn – fact is I come from a long line of stubborn – but this right here is living proof that stubborn and your Dionites ain't the same thing. So just humor me for a minute and pretend like I ain't a Dionite spy."

"Fine." She rolled her eyes. "I'm pretending."

"So what questions would you have if I wasn't a Dionite?"

"Alright, I'll play along. Did you see anybody else skulking through the ruins with you?"

"Not until your soldiers jumped me."

"What about on the road into town?"

"Quiet as church on a Saturday night. I ain't seen no-one in days."

"Why are you here?"

"Supplies, like I said."

"And why the hell should I believe you?"

"Because I don't know shit about what you're doing here. You say the Dionites are causing you trouble, I'll take your word for it. You think they're savages, I'll believe you. You got some kinda sacred Oracle keeps you safe and warm at night, gives you something to pray to or take signs from or decorate your Christmas trees with, lets you talk to the gods you're all so wound tight about, that's fine with me. You can bend down five times a day and pray towards your Oracle for all I care, but I like living wild and free, and last time I checked that ain't a sin."

"I'll tell you what's a sin." She was up in his face again,

hands trembling as they clutched her gun. "Letting savage swine like you run riot across the world, looting and pillaging and rutting like wild beasts out in the woods. We're rebuilding here. Someday there will be proper towns again, with schools and hospitals and safe streets. Children will get a proper education, and no-one will die from diseases we could have lived through before the fall. There will be lights in the streets and cars on the roads and healthy, happy people in a healthy, happy world, and that's going to happen because the Oracle was kept safe by people who knew how to listen to it, how to use what it says, not handed over to a bunch of wild-haired free-loving savages.

"I know a Dionite when I see one. Someday soon you'll let down your guard, you'll show the real creature playing at being civilized. And then we'll find out what you and your pals are up to next, and we'll be ready for them. Because civilization will be restored, no matter what you think."

Noah felt blasted by the vitriol in her voice, the passion in her eyes. Lost for words, he lifted his pick and got to work again.

That was the last time Burns spoke to him that day. He kept his head down and got on with his work. By the time the detail finished and the guards started marching them back towards the walls, dusk was falling and Noah was wearier than he'd been in weeks. The only thing worse than the thought of another day of work like that was the thought of being locked up in the cells again.

Vostok was with him as they passed through the gate, Burns glaring at Noah as he tramped past her. He caught the Russian guard's eye, nodded back towards the sergeant.

"You think she likes me?" he asked with a wink.

Vostok laughed his low, easy laugh.

"How much time she spends with you?" he said. "Must be love. Maybe she brings you flowers tomorrow, yes?"

CHAPTER 10
A HELPING HAND

THE NEXT DAY'S work detail was pretty much like the first. The guards clearly had a thorough, well ordered system for getting the inmates fed, into their shackles and out to work. Noah once again found himself separated from Iver, who had spent the night alternating between silence and wolf-like howls and so provided no new information. He was on a different chain from Blood Dog but in the same group, again led out through the side gate and around to clear the ruins surrounding the jail.

In his memory, Noah had cleared away most of a ruined house during the previous day's labor. It came as a huge disappointment to come in sight of it again and realize that it was still standing, just a corner carted off through all that back breaking work. But he set to it again, determined not to let a few walls get the best of him.

The soldiers who oversaw them in the jail and accompanied them on their work clearly had plenty of other duties, both inside and outside the town. Through the day Noah saw groups wandering around distant patches of ruins or up into the edges of the woods and hills beyond, always armed, always ready, always looking like they expected trouble to spring out on them at any moment. He'd seen them in town as well during the brief journey between the prison and the gate, watching the citizens about their business, stepping in at any sign of trouble. Their armor and weapons were a mish-mashed assortment of things left over from before the meteors and whatever could be cobbled together from what remained, as many wearing thickly padded jackets as had real body armor, a couple even dressed in ring-mail or metal plates dangling from cable ties. But all bore the symbol of Apollo, the drawn bow and arrow, and all wore the same distinctive red neck scarves.

Noah also thought he might have some idea what the Dionites looked like. Burns had talked about them as wild and savage looking, and while none of the prisoners looked too civilized there was a certain type who hung together in the feed hall and talked together on the chain gangs – men and women in loincloths and with plentiful tattoos. If they weren't some kind of gang then they were Apollo's most backward looking fashion trend. Treated particularly harshly by the guards and ostracized by the other half of the inmates, they were certainly looking like his best bet. If he could identify them for sure, then maybe he could find out a bit more about this place, enough to appease Burns and find a way out.

One thing he knew for sure – Blood Dog wasn't one of these Dionites. He had his own special place within the strange social hierarchy of the prison, watched carefully by everyone, avoided by most of his fellow inmates, but with others circling around him like vultures hoping for the scraps after his kills.

Today Blood Dog was in a particularly shitty mood. He laid waste to the ruins with a mad strength that Noah almost envied, slithers of brick and concrete flying like shrapnel all around him.

A woman on wheelbarrow detail lost control of her barrow on the rough ground and spilled broken bricks all around Blood Dog's feet. He leaped at her, fists flying, spitting the vilest curses Noah had ever heard. The woman darted away, her face a rictus of terror, and it was only when Blood Dog's chain ran up short that he was kept from chasing after her. He stopped for a moment, looking back at the two-foot iron peg with which the guards had fixed him to a spot, then went back to work, glaring around at everyone as he set to swinging once more with the pick.

"He bit a man's ear off last week," said Jen, the round faced woman next to Noah on the chain. "Spat it out into the face of one of the guards. Took six guards to restrain him, and I heard two of them are still in the infirmary."

"He always been this way?" Noah asked.

"More or less." Jen leaned on her shovel, glanced around in case the guards were watching, but they were too preoccupied to care about the prisoners going a little slow, half of them guarding a street thief while another patrol finished chasing his accomplice. "He's gotten worse the last few weeks on account of his trial's coming up. He's up for death, and no-one's taking odds against it."

"What did he do?" Noah wasn't really sure he wanted to know what atrocities his cellmate was capable of, not while there was no escaping him at night. But at the same time he couldn't resist scratching at the scab of curiosity.

"What didn't he do? Blood Dog ran half the crime in Apollo before Molly Burns brought him down. Ran guns, drugs, meds. Put the squeeze on businesses. Killed folks for money or for fun. They say he killed his first man when he was sixteen, sliced him open with a shard of glass. Maybe that's true and maybe it ain't, but criminal life got pretty exciting in Apollo after he arrived, both for good and for bad."

"He been inside long?"

"Long enough to kill five more, including a guard. That's

how everyone knows he's going to hang and burn. Everyone except Blood Dog at least. Though even he's sane enough that the prospect of a trial's turned him a little crazier."

As she spoke, Blood Dog picked up a chunk of masonry as broad as his own chest. He raised it above his head and then flung it at one of his fellow prisoners. The man only just jumped clear, the block smashing a wall next to where he'd stood. Even as the guards ran over to beat him down, Blood Dog laughed like a fierce jungle beast.

The guards beat Blood Dog until he stopped resisting, then they separated him off from the rest of his chain gang and three of them led him back in through the town gate.

Noah glanced around. There were only three guards now covering seventeen prisoners, plus the street thief the other patrol had brought in, a gangling youth with no shoes and an idiot grin. If there was ever a time to escape, this was it.

He waited until he was sure that the guards were preoccupied then shifted his chain, putting a link up on the wall he was breaking down.

"Won't do you no good," Jen said.

"You saying you ain't in?" Noah hadn't planned on springing anyone but himself, but better an accomplice than someone who might call the guards.

"I'll try anything." She shifted around to better block the guards' view of Noah. "You get them two links there, reckon we can both slide off this chain and be gone."

"Alright then." Noah hefted his pick, slammed it down against the chain. The brick beneath it crumbled but the metal barely showed a scratch.

"Keep going," Jen murmured. "No point giving up now."

Noah swung the pick again and again, hoping that he was doing more damage than it looked like.

"Hold a second," Jen said.

Noah looked around. The guard patrol that had brought

in the street thief was back, and they had another captive. Kicking and squirming in the grip of a muscled soldier was a scrawny teenage girl dressed in ragged clothes and with a mop of brown hair flying around her face.

"You know who that is?" Noah asked.

"Nope." Jen shook her head. "But the Elders said there were ten thousand souls in Apollo at the last census, and I sure as shit ain't had time to meet them all."

"I think she was following me the day I was brought in." Noah tilted his head, trying to get a better look past Burns. If she wasn't the same girl then, she was mighty similar looking.

"Reckon half the town will have been watching you," Jen said. "Gotta get our kicks somehow and seeing a Dionite brought in sometimes has to do."

Noah suddenly perked up. He'd been such an idiot. Why hadn't he just asked the other prisoners what he wanted to know? If his captors knew what a Dionite was, and the Dionites knew what a Dionite was, why wouldn't the other people around here?

"These Dionites," he said. "What are they-"

"Back to work prisoner," one of the patrol soldiers growled as they walked past.

Noah obediently got back to it, pick rising and falling on the pile of rubble and the chain draped across it. Was it his imagination or was he starting to wear through one side? He focused on the task rather than talking, not wanting to do anything that might risk drawing attention to him and Jen.

He kept his head down as Burns walked past them too, dragging the new prisoner by what passed for a collar on her stained and tattered t-shirt. Keeping a careful eye on them in case Burns came back, Noah swung his pick in a dramatic but ineffective display of work, hammering at broken and easily shifted debris for the biggest impression of labor.

To his surprise, Burns didn't drag the girl back to town or to some holding cell for an interrogation and a beating. Instead she dragged her aside into the relatively upright ruins of a garage.

"What you doing?" Jen hissed as he moved forward a few steps, the chain stretching out behind him, so he could spy on them through his own set of ruins.

"Just curious," he replied. Whether it was the curiosity of a man interested in a woman or of a prisoner wanting leverage over his captor Noah wasn't sure, but curiosity sure was the thing right now.

He'd half expected Burns to be laying down some sort of illicit beating, or shaking the girl down for bribes in return for letting her go. Sure, Burns had struck him so far as the upright type, and hearing her mentioned in relation to Blood Dog's downfall added to that image, but Noah's worldview held room for suspicion of everyone. There were no surprises left in the world, and very few righteous souls. Noah knew he wasn't among them, why expect any different from Burns?

Yet here was a surprise right before his eyes. The woman who had beaten him bloody, who had brought down the most dangerous killer in Apollo, was smoothing down the hair of a street urchin using her own neck scarf to wipe dirt and a smear of blood from the girl's face and examining her scrapes and bruises with a look of concern that Noah had previously thought beyond her. They were talking quietly to each other. He couldn't hear what it was about, but once she was done cleaning Burns pulled a loaf of flatbread and a couple of apples from a pouch on her belt and handed them over. The girl munched on an apple with such enthusiasm that Noah wondered if she'd eaten all week. He knew that desperate, empty feeling, and by the looks of her, the girl did too.

So this was the real Burns - not the angry woman who'd laid into him in an interrogation room, but someone caring and compassionate, maybe even one of the real good guys. It had been a long time since Noah had met one of the real good guys, and now he wanted to get to know her even more.

Burns glanced around, peering back towards where her fellow guards stood. Apparently satisfied that no-one was watching, she hugged the girl who squeezed her tightly back. Then Burns sent her scurrying off through the ruins back around the edge of town, away from their guard detail and the other patrol.

As she stepped out of the ruined garage, Burns glanced over towards the ruins where Noah stood. He ducked back behind the remains of a wall, then started pounding at it with his pick, determined to look busy.

She rounded the corner, stepped up next to Noah, and peered over his shoulder towards where she'd been a minute before. Then she turned to face him.

"Think you're smart, huh?" she said.

"My Mama told me so," Noah replied, trying to look innocent. He knew from past experience that he was no good at it, but practice made perfect, right? "But then our Mamas are biased, ain't they?" Her face told him she wasn't going for the innocent look- better try another move instead. "You got any kids, Sergeant Burns?"

He shot a pointed look back towards the ruined garage. Burns narrowed her eyes.

"Whatever you think you saw, you didn't." She looked from him to his chains and then down to Jen, who was trying very hard not to look like she was listening as she shoveled rubble into a barrow.

Burns squatted next to the chain, ran a finger along the battered link where Noah had been making his bid for freedom. Then she looked at the head of his pick, some points on its blade freshly gleaming where they'd been battered against other metal. She rose and leaned in close to Noah.

"I guess we both have secrets now," she murmured. "Let's keep it that way, huh?"

She turned and strode off back towards the other guards, calling out over her shoulder.

"I'll be keeping a close eye on you two."

"Nice work, lover boy." Now it was Jen's turn to glare at Noah.

He shrugged.

"Are you any less free than you were this morning?" he asked.

"I suppose not." She hefted a last shovel of rubble into the barrow, looked around for someone to wheel it away. "But what was all the whispering about?"

"Reckon I'm in love," Noah said.

"And her?"

"Reckon she's in hate. But I'll grow on her."

"And if you don't?"

"Then how do you feel about walks under starlight?"

Jen glanced over at a guard striding angrily towards them, lifted her shovel and moved as far as she could from Noah.

"Reckon I feel like digging."

CHAPTER 11
LAST NIGHT

Noah's idea to ask other prisoners about the Dionites had arrived at a lousy time. Blood Dog had carried on picking fights after they brought him back to the jail, putting two more inmates in the infirmary and leaving evidence in the form of bloodstains on the canteen floor.

This had put all the guards on edge. They'd vented their tensions by beating down on any hint of trouble, from fights between prisoners to inmates looking at them funny. The prisoners, feeling the pressure of scrutiny and the pain of the guards' clubs, had closed down into their defensive cliques, no-one talking to anyone who wasn't already in their gang. And Noah was in a gang of one.

It didn't help that Burns was making a point of watching him and Jen, and even got other officers in on it.

"I do not know what you do to her," Vostok said as Noah passed him in the hall, "but Sergeant Burns, she has us all on you now, yes?"

He laughed and slapped Noah on the shoulder, though Noah didn't see much that was funny about it himself.

"Sounds about right," he agreed.

Vostok seemed a decent guy, but he was still undoubtedly a guard. Two minutes later, Noah saw him hit a guy for refusing to get back into line. He figured that was what this place did to you - if it didn't make you untrustworthy it made you untrusting, and either way it was just making you human. The good thing about prison was that there were no niceties painted over the top, creating the illusion that everything was happy and fluffy.

Of course, the bad thing about prison was that there were no niceties painted over the top, keeping folks from screaming at each other or beating on each other or stealing each other's food in the lunch line. The only thing holding back that barely contained layer of violence and mayhem was the threat of more violence and mayhem, which didn't exactly set the tone for fun and relaxation.

As he sat alone in his corner of the canteen, eating a stew that was more grit than vegetable and drinking water the guards had probably spat in, Noah watched the other inmates, trying to work out his next move, or at least what he could learn that might give him an edge. Knowledge was power, Mama used to say, and that was why she'd never put him or Jeb or Pete through school. She didn't want the authorities getting power over her sons by planting their sorts of knowledge into their heads. She wanted them to learn things that mattered, things that were real, and above all she taught them to keep learning.

So, Noah sat and watched. He was good at watching.

When he was a kid he'd had a dream that his father was some kind of spy. After all, he worked for the government, and whatever he did it was all very secretive. It took him away from home for weeks at a time, and when he returned he couldn't talk about what he'd done. That was something he impressed on the Brennan boys time and again - Pa worked with secret things and it was important, but he couldn't tell them about it.

Then he'd started reading thrillers, the same ones Pa kept on the shelves, and suddenly it all made sense. These secret agents and investigators, they were always traveling, always away from home, always doing things they couldn't talk about. They had to be spies. Pa had to be a spy. And like so many impressionable kids, Noah wanted to be like the man in his life. So he wanted to be a spy.

He raced through all those thrillers, learning as much craft as he could from them. He practiced it around town, watching folks covertly, following them up the street until they caught sight of him and told him to buzz off. Then he got on the internet and read all about spy craft and secret agents. It turned out that some of what was in the books wasn't quite right. In fact, it turned out that spying was mostly pretty boring, and the skills involved didn't seem a whole lot like the ones his Pa had. Whereas space shuttle engineers and the guys who built monster trucks, they had the real exciting jobs. Maybe he'd work with engines.

Thus ended young Noah Brennan's brief dreams of being a secret agent. But some of the skills stuck, and one of those was watching people, observing without drawing attention. He hunched over his stew and watched the canteen.

Blood Dog's friends were looking twitchy. Their leader wasn't with them and that was giving them a taste of what was to come. They eyed each other with suspicion, but showed downright hostility towards the wider world, a world that was closing in, not giving them the safe space they were used to with their boss around.

Jen seemed to be part of an Apollo town crew, like Blood Dog but not his gang. They'd dug in deepest in this defensive game of keeping heads down and weathering the day's storm. The street thief who the patrol had brought round to the chain guards today, the one with the idiot look and the awkward limbs, was in among that crew, which told Noah something about Burns' friend. She fit into the crime life of Apollo, but not the full-on thuggery of the town's Blood Dogs. Why Burns would help even such a low level criminal was an intriguing question.

Noah finished his stew and pushed the bowl away then picked up an apple. On close inspection it was worm-eaten and old enough to have gotten on the dried out and wrinkled side. But food was still food, and no-one was going to throw him a can of beans or a leg of fresh roasted lamb. Besides, if it was good enough for worms it was good enough for him, right?

He took a bite, remembered that worms would eat dirt, but kept on chewing.

While he ate, he watched the folks at the next table over. These were among the ones he'd pegged as Dionites, with all the bare flesh and tattoos. It flickered across his mind that Blood Dog and Burns both had tattoos too, but that didn't seem like much of a connection. Blood Dog's were crude, angry things. Burns' at least shared beauty with the pictures like these folks wore, but they lacked their smooth flow or focus on plants and animals. These folks had a real back to nature theme in their tats, lots of trees and free flying birds and coiling snakes.

Then it struck him, looking at a row of them, all hunched over and with their backs turned to him. The snakes weren't just a theme, they were a pattern, a symbol, the thing to make them stand out. Though the designs were different - some coiled around trees, some rising to strike, some just draped over their skin - there was a snake on the right shoulder of every man and woman at that table.

His apple finished, Noah got up and walked around the other side of the Dionites on his way to return his tray. Sure enough, the folks along this side had snakes on their right shoulders too.

Now all he needed to do was find Burns and show her

that he didn't have the snake. It might not get him a get out of jail free, but at least it might get him out of the unanswerable questions, make a start on getting him released.

He put his tray on the counter and headed back towards his cell, humming a tune to himself.

That humming lasted as far as the cell door and the guard who stood there, key in hand, waiting to let Noah in. She looked grim as the prison walls.

"They giving us our own doorman now?" Noah asked, trying to keep his spirits up. But just seeing that tiny, cramped space, never mind the thought of being locked back inside, made his guts clench and his brain spin with dread.

"Shut up and get inside." The guard opened the door, shoved him through and hurriedly swung the door shut again.

Looking back, Noah couldn't help but notice that the rest of the cells were still open, the inmates not yet locked down for the night. He didn't think that this extra security came on account of him, but it was sure going to mess with his state of mind.

Blood Dog stood in the corner of the cell, smashing his fist repeatedly against the same stretch of wall.

"Fuckers," he growled. "Fuckers. Fuckers. Fuckers. Fuckers."

Noah stepped over to the bunks as quietly as he could. He could hardly avoid being seen in a seven foot cell, but he could at least try not to disturb the lunatic who bit off other men's ears and slit their throats with glass.

Remembering the importance of not upsetting his cellmate, he looked cautiously around for the bike magazine. It lay in the corner of the cell, shredded into tiny scraps. The sight of Blood Dog's only comfort torn to pieces made Noah's blood run cold. If someone had done that to piss the monster off, then it was bad news. If Blood Dog had done it himself then it was appalling.

"Think they can put me on trial?" Blood Dog said, his fist hitting the wall again. Dust danced from the concrete. "Think they can kill me, the mother-fuckers? Well that ain't how it works, is it?"

When Noah stayed silent Blood Dog turned his eyes on him. The anger in those eyes made the blood pound in Noah's ears.

"I said is it?" Blood Dog said.

"No sir," Noah replied.

"Sir?' Blood Dog said, stepping away from the wall. "Who you sir'ing? You trying to be funny again?"

"No," Noah replied. "Nothing funny here."

Never had he spoken a truer word.

"No one makes fun of me," Blood Dog said. "No-one fucks with me. No-one kills me. You know why?"

Noah shook his head, sank onto his bunk and tried to back out of sight as Blood Dog approached.

"Cause I ain't never found no-one I can't fuck or kill," Blood Dog replied. "Girls, guards, gangsters, funny motherfuckers in prison cells. Everyone gives it up to Blood Dog in the end, one way or another."

Blood Dog tugged at his crotch as he stared down at Noah.

"Mother-fucking elders think they're gonna kill me," he continued. "Stand me up in front of some shitty-ass lawyer, spout some laws and charges, then string me up. But that ain't gonna happen. They know it. I know it. This time tomorrow I'll be back in my cell. And someday soon, when I get out of here, I'm gonna kill every last fucking elder."

The room was closing in around Noah. His heart felt like it was being squeezed in a fist, pressure building, blood racing. He was trapped, surrounded on every side, concrete behind and to left and right, Blood Dog looming like a wall of flesh in the front of his vision.

"Won't just be them though, wise guy." Blood Dog looked down at him with an intensity Noah could only hope was hate. "Cause there ain't nothing in the world I can't kill or fuck."

Footsteps were approaching along the walkway, footsteps and the rattle of keys. Noah's breath was getting fast and shallow, his head spinning as the ceiling loomed down upon him, shadows closing in from every part of the room.

"Gonna kill those elders," Blood Dog growled. "Gonna kill the guards. Gonna kill that bitch Burns who put me in this place. Question now is, what am I gonna do with you?"

Blood Dog grabbed Noah by the throat, lifted him up against the bunks. His hand tightened and Noah choked, gasping desperately for air. He looked down at Blood Dog's mad eyes, felt his own hands and feet twitching as he fought to stay still, not to struggle, to stay calm for the guards who were coming. Weren't they coming, hadn't he heard them coming?

The moment stretched out like a shadow spreading across Noah's world.

Then a metal club clanged against the bars and a key rattled in the lock.

"Put him down Blood Dog." Burns stood in the doorway, club raised ready for trouble. She almost seemed to be smiling. "There's a cell waiting for you down at the Council Chambers."

Blood Dog's hand disappeared from around Noah's throat and he fell sprawling on the floor, panting for breath.

Burns slapped manacles shut around Blood Dog's wrists and ankles, the chains cutting his strides to a slow shuffle. As he was led out the door he turned back to look at Noah.

"Fuck or kill," Blood Dog said. "Your choice."

As other guards led the prisoner away, Burns turned to lock the cell door. She looked down at Noah.

"You alright there?" she asked. "Need the infirmary?"

Noah shook his head.

"Fine," he gasped. "Just need a minute."

He tried to push himself manfully to his feet, failed, instead settled for what he hoped was a casual sprawl against the bottom bunk.

He doubted he was fooling anybody.

"He'll be back for one more night," Burns said. "Sure you don't want to tell me something, get yourself a different cell?"

"I ain't a Dionite," Noah rasped, gathering his thoughts ready to explain.

She shook her head.

"Whatever." And then she too was off.

Noah slid down to the floor, looking up at as much open space as the cell could hold, trying to get his breathing steady.

One more night.

Fuck or kill.

His whole body trembled in fear. He felt like he might break down crying, or burst out screaming like Iver.

He really, really needed to get out of this place.

CHAPTER 12
SMALL WORLDS

Noah wasn't sure how long he lay on the cell floor, first trying to get some control over the whirl of panic in his mind, then—when that proved futile—giving in and letting it consume him. Sometimes you had to give in to the chaos to come out on the other side. Sometimes you had to live with the pain to heal.

And sometimes you just had to lie on the floor, in the dried out remains of your own old vomit, letting the thoughts fly by. Because if you didn't, then those thoughts would batter you down.

Night had fallen by the time the thoughts settled and Noah once again found himself in control. The darkness probably helped - it was harder to feel oppressed by the close concrete walls when you couldn't see them. That was one of the reasons he'd always liked the stars, they were so damn far away they became a sign of the vastness above him, an emptiness so broad he could never reach its limits. His Pa had bought him a star chart once, brought it back from one of his work trips, and talked excitedly about how certain he was that man would reach the stars someday. That dream was shot to shit now - mankind could barely wipe its own collective ass, never mind pull together the technology to get off of the ruined Earth. But that star chart had made Noah's room feel bigger when he was a kid, just like the darkness made his cell feel bigger now.

He got up, stumbled over to the corner and took a piss in the cracked and grubby john. That at least was one discomfort he could relieve.

That done, it was time to come up with a plan. It didn't need to be a good plan, not yet. Sometimes just having a plan and acting on it got you going, led towards working out the real plan. Sometimes those in between plans even worked out, though sometimes they just led to slightly scratched chains and no kind of progress.

"What we gonna do then?" He reached down, patted the empty air in his holster. He'd never noticed how much comfort he took in Bourne, how much saner he felt talking to the pistol than muttering to himself. If that was crazy then at least being crazy was better than being Blood Dog's bitch.

Of course, the two might not be mutually exclusive if he didn't work out some way clear of this mess.

He figured he must have missed a good stretch of the evening because the cells around him had mostly fallen quiet. The one voice still muttering away was the one he wanted to hear, and that was Iver.

In the absence of a good plan he was shifting back to the one he'd been working on, just at a faster pace. Learn as much as he could about the Dionites, get Burns to question him again, and prove to her that he wasn't one of them. If Iver let slip something she wanted to hear about these people then, even better. Though Noah didn't reckon folks told Iver much they weren't happy for him to share with the sky, the walls, half the prison, and the pixies dancing inside his own head.

"Phalanges, metacarpals, carpals…" Iver was muttering to himself, head pressed against the bars.

"Hey, Iver," Noah hissed, settling down on the floor by

the door of his own cell, looking across the space between them.

"Busy." Iver held up a hand. "Temporal, zygomatic, maxilla…dammit, I missed some I missed some, it's all gone I missed some…"

He started rocking back and forth, knocking his forehead against the bars, dreadlocks flapping like tentacles on some sad sea monster.

"It's OK Iver," Noah said. "That's in the past. You've got the Dionites now, and they're coming to save you, right?"

"They're coming for me?" Iver looked up with a big innocent smile, childlike, and radiant.

"That's right," Noah said. "Least that's what I heard. The chief or mayor or someone's sending them to get you."

"Oh no," Iver said. "No chiefs. No mayors. No presidents or kings or CEOs. Who needs rulers and lawyers and laws when you can be free in the forest, when you can live back with nature like Gaia intended, when you all live as one, one mind, one body, one heart, one intention and happiness, oh yes."

"So you folks live in the woods?" Noah said.

"Oh yes."

Iver sighed and lay back on the concrete floor of his cell, up against the bars so that he was staring through the murky ceiling glass above them and at the stars beyond. He seemed to have almost drifted away, then just as Noah was wondering what to ask next he started up again.

"I used to be like this place, all rules and regulations and order. I thought I had to put everything into a neatly structured box. My mind was one neatly structured pile of boxes, like a shopping aisle not a human brain. And I've seen inside brains. We try to pin them down, to order them and separate them and say 'this is the frontal lobe, it does reasoning; this is the occipital lobe, it does vision.' But that's not how we work, man. Not people and not brains. It's all connected, all a tangled and beautiful collection of connections. There's more to a mind than just a brain, there's the soul as well. And each soul isn't separate, it's part of the whole world, living and loving together. The Tribe understands that. The Tribe has had their eyes opened to what it is to be truly human. No leaders, no commanders, all working together."

"The tribe being the Dionites?" Noah could see the sense in it all. Those people with their tattoos of nature, living out in the woods, thinking hippie thoughts like Iver here.

"Oh yes," Iver said. "We live the happy life, not the ordered life."

Noah tapped his fingers against the empty holster. He needed a way to turn this around, to lead Iver's thoughts towards something more specific, more useful. An aim or a plan, the sort of stuff Burns had wanted to get out of him. He could hardly say 'hey Iver, you guys planning to steal these people's oracle? How's that gonna go down?' But Iver did like to talk, and maybe if he started big he could steer him around to the details.

It was hard to be patient given what was on the line, but at least a little patience was going to be needed.

"So you folks have got it worked out, huh?" he said. "You understand the answers?"

"Can anyone really understand the answers?" Iver said, to Noah's intense irritation. "We can only work towards them, for life is a journey. I thought I had the answers, laid bare with my scalpel and with my bank account. But I was wrong, so very wrong. We are only steps along the path. Even when we find Astra, that'll only be one more step along the way."

"Astra?" Noah asked. "What's Astra?"

"Astra is the dream. Astra is the hope. Astra is what we

seek to unshackle us from the ruins of the past and propel us into the future. Astra is not all that matters, but Astra is the goal, the great step forward, the hope for love and unity and a clearer world. If we are worthy, if we live freely and well, if we do not allow ourselves to be bound by laws and by walls, then maybe one day we will find it..."

Iver's voice trailed off. Noah lay in the silence, pondering this new detail, this new name. Astra. It could be anything. Could be a person or a place or an idea or just some broken down old car that Iver associated with his own hippie dreams of the future. But it seemed to matter to him, and maybe the rest of the Dionites. If it meant something to Burns then maybe knowing that the Dionites were after it could be his out. But if it meant nothing to her then he needed to know more.

This whole business was like trying to get spares for an engine when he didn't even know what sort of car it came from. He just had to keep collecting as many bits as he could and hope that some of them fitted into the spaces in the end.

"Hey man, what's your name?" Iver peered through the bars straight across at Noah. There was a clarity to his voice, a focus in his expression that Noah had never seen there before.

"Noah. My name's Noah."

"Does that make this your ark?" Iver asked. "You got two rabbits in there? Two snakes? Two doves?"

Noah had heard the joke a thousand times and he'd grown to hate it. But here in jail, where he faced only horrors and hard labor, it was a relief to hear anything even close to funny. And coming from Iver it was hard to hear any malicious intent in the words or to react with resentment.

To Noah's surprise he found himself laughing. And as the sound rippled through his body, shaking loose all the tensions of the previous days, something broke within him. As if from nowhere laughter turned into tears and he trembled on the cold concrete, overcome by it all. A great bout of sobbing broke forth from him, and when it ended he was the most relaxed he'd felt in years.

"Shit, but I needed that," he said, sniffing and wiping the tears from his face. It felt childish and absurd for a grown man to break down like that, but it felt strangely satisfying too.

"We all do, sometimes," Iver said. "It's OK to feel, man. I had to learn that too."

Iver poked his arm between the bars, splayed fingers reaching out across the space between them. Noah did the same, just wanting some human contact that didn't come with menaces or a beating. He couldn't quite reach, their fingertips straining, only inches apart. Noah felt himself knotting up again in frustration, but then he looked at the smile on Iver's face and he realized that this was enough.

"That's it man," Iver said. "Give in to the good as well as the bad."

Noah drew back his arm, settled down with a contented sigh. He wouldn't have gone so far as to say that it felt good to be alive, but it sure didn't feel half so hideous anymore.

"You got a last name Noah?" Iver asked.

"Brennan." Noah said. "Noah Brennan."

Iver burst out laughing. There was a madness to the sound, his mind slipping back into itself again.

"What's so funny?" Noah asked.

"I knew a Brennan," Iver said. "Man who mattered. Man who made things different. More the outdoors type though. With the tracking and the trapping in between the other bits, not your fighting and smuggling and Blood Dog death dance crime dance city dance antics. Not an Apollo man. No no no."

"You've got me wrong, Iver," Noah said, once again realizing too late where he should have started the whole mad conversation. "I ain't one of these Apollo folks. I'm an outdoorsman, a Tennessee man, like my Pa before him and his Pa before him."

"Brennan I knew was a Tennessee man too," Iver said. "Must be a Tennessee thing. Like mockingbirds and country songs and dead Indians. Poor Indians, all trailing off into tears, all because the white man couldn't live right by others never mind by nature. We should have listened, should have lived, should have saved ourselves from our doom, our moon doom, doom moon, moon moon silvery moon two eyes a nose and a mouth..."

"Guess so."

"Old silvery Tom Brennan," Iver murmured.

Noah jolted upright at the sound of his Pa's name.

"Tom Brennan?" he asked. "You knew an outdoors guy from Tennessee called Tom Brennan?"

"Uhuh," Iver murmured. "Looked a little like you too. All...moon eyed, doom eyed, you know? Like the weight of the world wearing down on him. Like he might just let it grind him into dust. Or moon fragments, scattered across the sky. One, two, three, four, five..."

Iver raised a finger, apparently counting the endless bright fragments in the haze of the meteor belt across the southern sky. But Noah didn't care about moon rocks right now.

"Iver, listen to me, look at me," he said. "This Tom Brennan, might be that was my Pa. Did you meet him after everything fell apart? Do you know where he was when it all went down? Do you know where he went?"

But Iver was gone, vanished into the sky and the numbers and whatever dreams went on in the back of his head. Noah tried to get more out of him, but it was no use.

He lay back himself and looked up at the stars. Had his father really lived through the apocalypse? Did he have some connection to Iver and his Dionites? It was a crazy thought, but this was a crazy world, a baboon in Virginia sort of world, a world where damn near anything could happen.

Whatever tomorrow held, tonight he didn't want to retreat back into the confines of his cell. He dragged his mattress from the bed and put it down next to the door so that he could look up through the bars at the stars. He lay back, hands behind his head, and let the sound of Iver's counting lull him to sleep.

CHAPTER 13
BLOOD

If the night had been one of fear and then hope, the next morning was one of terrible disappointment. Any kind of plan to get out of his cell, and thus away from Blood Dog, relied on Noah getting ahold of Sergeant Burns, convincing her that he wasn't a Dionite and maybe even sharing some knowledge he'd gained about them. She seemed like a woman who prized information - why else had she worked so hard to get it out of him? Maybe she'd be interested in Iver's talk of Astra.

It was a long shot, but it was the only one he had.

Unfortunately, as the guards led him from his cell down towards the canteen for his breakfast and chains, there was no sign of Sergeant Burns.

"Excuse me." He took a chance on pausing by the guard room that looked onto the main hallway, addressing the back of the nearest guard. "Is Sergeant Burns here? I believe I've got some information that might interest her."

The man turned around and Noah recognized Lieutenant Poulson, the angry looking guy who'd led his capture. Poulson didn't look any happier to see Noah now than he had in the school library.

"Sergeant Burns is not here," Poulson said. "Will not be all day."

"Perhaps you could pass on a message?" Noah said. "I think she'll want to know—"

"You think you have something more urgent than Council business?" Poulson sneered. "Get back into your place. You won't get out of work this easily."

"But I—"

"Go." Poulson turned away, gestured one of the other guards to move Noah along.

As Noah turned, he caught a glimpse of the far wall inside the guard room. It was lined with guns, bows, and swords. One weapon in particular stood out.

"Hey, that's my pistol," he said, forgetting himself in the excitement of spotting Bourne. Then the guard stepped up, club raised, and Noah hurried along.

If he had believed in omens, then he would have taken seeing Bourne as a good one. And though he might not be superstitious, the boost of knowing where his traveling companion was being held helped carry him through the morning, breaking rocks and keeping an eye out for the return of Burns. His bruises were fading and though his muscles ached from the labor he was now well into the rhythm of it, finding ways to get the most done for the least strain on his body. It wasn't much to take satisfaction in, but it was something.

He sang to himself as he worked, half-remembered rock songs he'd listened to with Jeb and Pete. He got through a few renditions of 'The Boys Are Back In Town,' sang the chorus of 'Wheels On Fire' until Jen yelled at him to shut the hell up. He was halfway through 'Sweet Home Alabama' when Burns appeared around the corner of the building. He lifted his voice in celebration, bellowing out the chorus, getting not just her attention but, of all the unexpected wonders, a smile.

"You got a moment sergeant?" he called out.

"Sorry prisoner, no can do." She gestured back towards town. "Trial's still on and I don't want to miss the best bit."

"But it's about–"

"Later," she said, turning and striding towards the gate. "The one thing the gods have given you is time."

Noah turned back to his work, but he didn't feel much like singing anymore. He'd gotten his hopes up that if he just saw Burns, he could talk his way out of the cell today. But she had other duties to perform, marching and guarding and maybe bearing witness against the murderer she'd locked Noah up with. If she was busy all day, then it might be tomorrow before she got to him, or the day after, and meanwhile Blood Dog would be coming back.

He felt like his guts had been pressed down into the bottom of his body, crushed beneath some terrible weight. He'd never been much for praying, not like his Mama had, but right then he could almost have pleaded with whatever was out there, looking over this terrible and indifferent world.

Instead, he swung his pick, feeling every twinge of his muscles as he did – the rhythm was gone.

Night was falling. The sound of boots tramped up the steps from the prison's ground floor and along the walkway towards Noah's cell. He opened his eyes, stared at the bunk above him, nausea rising from the pit of his stomach.

He'd failed. He'd found no way out, no way clear of this place, and now those footsteps could announce only one thing – Blood Dog's return.

"Iver," he called out, desperate for some shred of comfort,

the sound of a friendly voice.

"I'm here," Iver replied. "Here and there and everywhere."

"That Tom Brennan you knew," Noah said. "What sort of man was he? What sort of things did he-"

A guard slid the key into the cell door. Noah fell silent, slid as far as he could into the shadows cast by the upper bunk.

The door swung open, but instead of Blood Dog's confident footsteps Noah heard sounds of violence approaching down the hallway, up the stairs and along the walkway. Grunts and groans, the thud of clubs against flesh, curses and howls and intermittent footsteps.

Finally, a cluster of guards appeared with Blood Dog at their center. There was a large bruise on the side of his head, more on his arms, and blood trickled from between his lips. The guards weren't in much better shape. Two had bloody noses, and Vostok was wincing as he helped haul the prisoner through the door and fling him down in the cell.

"You'll never kill me!" Blood Dog yelled as he sprawled on the floor, kicking and struggling against the rope that bound his hands behind his back.

"That's not what the Council say," Vostok replied. "They say we hang you tomorrow, and good riddance to such filth."

He slammed the door shut and the key turned in the lock once more. The guards disappeared down the walkway and away.

Blood Dog writhed on the floor some more, apparently oblivious to Noah's presence. With a little effort, he got up onto his knees. He stayed like that, arms straining, muscles bulging in his shoulders until there was a snap and the rope binding his wrists gave way.

"You can't keep me, see?" he yelled, throwing the tattered ends of rope out through the bars. "You can't hold me in here. I'll kill you all! All except that bitch Burns. Her I'll fuck and I'll kill and I'll fuck some more, and I'll strangle your fucking Council with the last shreds of her whore guts. You hear me?"

He grabbed hold of the bars, shook them so violently that Noah thought they might break out of the concrete or snap in Blood Dog's hands. Noah wouldn't have minded that, wouldn't have minded at all. If the brute got out of the cell then he had other targets, might find someone else to destroy before he remembered Noah.

No such luck. Blood Dog turned away from the bars, his whole body heaving with rage, his breath blasting fierce and loud like a bellows in a blacksmith's shop. He ran over to the toilet bowl and kicked it. The porcelain exploded into white shards, spattering the wall with water. More trickled from the broken end of the inlet pipe.

"Fuck you!" Blood Dog screamed it like a war cry, like a mantra that might call down the boon of some angry, hate-filled god. "Fuck you!"

He grabbed his mattress and ripped it in half, flung the two parts across the cell. Fragments of cotton drifted in the air.

Through the wire mesh of the bunk, Blood Dog stared down at Noah. His face filled with malevolent glee.

"I forgot about you, wise guy." Blood Dog reached down and started to unbuckle his belt. "You going to play nice, or am I going to have kill you too before I fuck you?"

Noah wasn't scared of a fight, but he'd tried to avoid a confrontation with this man mountain, because this was one he had little chance of winning. But little chance was better than handing himself over to be raped by some murdering asshole. Never let it be said that the Brennan boys gave in without a fight.

He lashed out with his foot, straight into Blood Dog's

crotch. Blood Dog's fingers took some of the force of the blow, but he still bent over, wheezing and grimacing.

Noah scrambled out from the bunks and across the room. He grabbed the sharpest shard of the toilet bowl he could see. Broken pottery wasn't much of a blade, but if you stabbed hard enough any point could take out an eye.

He turned as Blood Dog lumbered over to him, ducked a swing of the vast man's arms and dodged out behind him, slashing with the shard as he went. His heart was beating like a drum, a thudding that filled his ears, filled his world with the echo of his own terror.

Blood Dog turned again. For all his size he wasn't slow. His kick caught Noah behind the knee and he only just managed to keep his feet. A slab of hand grabbed him by the arm, yanked him over to Blood Dog.

Pulled in close, Noah jabbed with the piece of pottery, stabbing it as hard as he could into the arm that had hold of his own. Blood spurted from a tattoo of a huge breasted woman.

Blood Dog yelled in pain and let go of Noah's arm. But his other fist hit Noah in the chest, sending him reeling back against the bunks. The sound of his racing heartbeat was broken by something deeper and he wondered what vital part of him had just broken.

He dodged clear as Blood Dog descended on him again, but there were only so many places he could go in a seven foot cell. A blow numbed his arm and the shard of broken toilet bowl slipped through his useless fingers, shattering on the floor. Another blow smashed into his face and the whole world went hazy. He stumbled, was lifted from his feet by a giant hand. Black spots danced across his vision and his mouth filled with the salt taste of blood.

Blood Dog had hold of him again, was pressing him up against the frame of the bunks, one hand around Noah's throat, the other yanking at his pants.

Another dull, irregular thud broke the rhythm of his heart beating in his ears. How much could there be left working inside him? How many more things would break before this was over?

Iver was screaming something from the cell next door, but it was too late for help.

The whole cell seemed to shake with the next thud, and Noah hoped this meant he was falling unconscious. But instead he fell to the ground as Blood Dog let him go.

"What the fuck?" Blood Dog said as he stared out through the bars of the door.

Lying on the ground next to the bunks, some small, desperate part of Noah took over, an instinct to hide, to delay the inevitable by whatever fragments of a moment he could. With what little strength he had he slid under the bed, into the darkest shadow of an already dark room. His shirt was quickly soaked by water from the broken toilet pipe, but that was nothing compared with the horror of Blood Dog still looming in the center of the room, still staring out through bars.

Then came a roar like a meteorite crashing to Earth and Noah's whole world exploded.

CHAPTER 14
AMIDST THE RUINS

THE RINGING FILLED Noah's mind, filled his whole world. He clasped his hands over his ears, trying to shut it out, only to find that the ringing came from within.

Slowly he opened his eyes, saw the one thing he had most feared - Blood Dog staring right back at him. He shrank back against the wall, instinct rather than reason pushing him as far from his tormentor as possible.

But there was something wrong with Blood Dog's face. The hate was gone from his eyes, replaced by an unblinking emptiness. And as Noah stared at the sight in front of him, he realized that the top of the murderer's tattooed head had been replaced by a bloody, broken mess.

Cautiously, Noah wriggled his way back to the edge of the bed and peered from underneath it. Sure enough, Blood Dog lay dead, his head caved in, arms and legs torn and tangled, his body half buried beneath broken pieces of concrete.

But Blood Dog wasn't the only hateful thing lying ruined on the floor of the cell. The door had fallen from its hinges, its bars buckled and twisted. Most of the wall between his cell and Iver's had been destroyed, along with a huge chunk of the exterior wall and half of the ceiling.

As the ringing in his ears faded it was replaced with the

sound of alarm bells, women and men shouting, feet running, blows being traded with fists or clubs or both.

He stumbled to his feet, half choked on a mixture of brick dust and smoke. Looking down he could hardly believe that he was almost unscathed by the blast that had destroyed his cell and his cellmate with it. A sliver of something had cut the back of his hand but that was the extent of any injury. The iron bed frame, itself battered and piled high with rubble, had protected him from the blast.

Iver hadn't been so lucky. He lay slumped against the wall of his cell, blood running from a head wound and a shard of metal protruding from his chest. Noah clambered over the rubble, knelt down beside him.

"Iver?" he said, barely able to hear himself between the ringing and the sounds of distant violence. "Iver, you still there?"

Iver lifted his head. The pupil of one eye looked larger than the other. Blood bubbled between his pale lips.

"Tommy Brennan," he spluttered, a distant look in his eyes. "How you been Tommy Brennan? Did you fetch me a suture?"

"Not Tom Brennan. I'm Noah, remember? And you're going to tell me all about Tom Brennan, just as soon as I get you out of here."

"Going nowhere," Iver said, looking down at himself. He raised one hand to the side of his head, gingerly touched the wound there. "Sucking chest wound. Collapsed lung. Fractured skull and inevitable concussion."

"It ain't that bad," Noah said, his voice rising with desperation. He didn't want Iver to die. He wanted him to tell him about his Pa, about whether he had been through here, whether he was still alive after all these years. But as much as that, he didn't want to see a good guy die in the same squalor and ruin as Blood Dog. A good guy who had seen him through, who had given him hope. "I can get you out of here. Just let me find something for bandages."

"Patient has significant blood loss," Iver muttered.

"I wouldn't say significant," Noah said. But it wasn't just water soaking his clothes any more. There was a pool of blood spreading out around Iver, soaking into Noah's pants, hot and wet and awful.

"Flesh cold," Iver said. "He's going into shock. Nurse, fetch twenty cc's of... twenty cc's of..."

With one last gasp Iver's head slumped forward and he fell silent.

"Iver," Noah said. "Iver, come on buddy."

He reached for Iver's neck, felt for any kind of pulse. But as he expected, there was nothing.

"Goddammit." Noah rose to his feet, took a good look around. To his right, through the hole in the prison wall, a heap of rubble lay in the road below. People were shouting and guns firing somewhere out in the night.

To his left, the prison was in uproar. Whatever had hit the building, it had hit some of the cells hard enough to free their inmates, who were now escaping through broken doors and off down the hall or clambering through holes in the wall and away into the distance. The rest of the prisoners were pleading or yelling at them, desperate to be let out themselves. They waved their arms through the bars, screamed and shouted and begged.

What Noah couldn't see was any sign of guards.

That was when the reality of his situation struck him. Here was what he wanted, the thing he'd been looking for from the moment Poulson dragged him into this concrete hell – a way out.

He stumbled over patches of rubble to the hole in the wall. As he did, another lump of concrete fell from the ceiling, missing him by half a foot. Better to get moving before the whole place fell down around his ears.

He perched at the edge of the gap, swung one leg out and down. It would be a bit of a drop, and days of hard labor had left his legs stiff as a teenage boy on prom night, so it wasn't going to be the most graceful of exits. But even if he fell on his ass at least he'd be out, and what was a couple more bruises?

A chunk of rubble slid away, clattered down the remaining debris, as pieces of masonry smashed against each other before settling on the uneven and shadow-strewn ground.

A couple of bruises or a cracked skull.

"It's this or more beatings," Noah said, reaching down to his holster for comfort.

His empty holster.

He glanced back toward the prison hall and the guard room at the far end. No guards meant no-one guarding that room. Sure, they might have taken Bourne with them, but what if they hadn't. Bourne was his lifeline, a way of scaring off robbers, of intimidating cut-price traders, of chasing away hungry critters in the night. OK, so the last one would only work if he could find some bullets, but there was always hope, right?

And he hated to admit it, but life just wasn't the same with an empty space in the holster on his thigh.

"Goddammit." He pulled his aching leg back up over the edge, hauled himself to his feet. Another chunk of rubble fell down on the far side of the cell. Clangs and excited cries rang from the prison hall below. "Better be quick about this."

He ran out of the cell and along the walkway. If the past half hour had given him one thing it was adrenaline, and his body was still working for all it was worth, muscles straining through the pain and exhaustion. He took the steps down two at a time, almost falling over his own feet as he hit the ground, and carried on running.

Down here he could see that not all of the inmates had fled. A growing number, all marked with Dionite snake tattoos, had picked up chunks of broken bed frames or bars from fallen doors and were using them as improvised picks and levers to bust open their comrades' cells. Maybe this whole mess was the rescue Iver had been waiting for. If so, then it was a shitty way for it to go down for him, blown to hell by his own tribesmen, just a casualty in their bid to free the rest of their mob. It seemed maybe Iver had chosen the wrong side.

At least the Dionites seemed happy to leave Noah to his business - the business of getting armed and then the hell out of here. He ran from the main hall into the corridor that led to the guard room door and stopped.

It was locked. The handle rattled futilely as Noah tried to open it. But locked as it was, sturdy as it might once have been, this was still a door in the rough end of a busted up town, and one that clearly hadn't been new when things went to hell. The guards apparently didn't know much about looking after a building - they'd let woodworm eat into parts of the frame, and an inept repair job around the lock had left joints between old and new wood that would make the door vulnerable.

"Cowboys." Noah stepped back and slammed his foot against the door. He did it again and again. It had always worked the first time in movies, at least the ones he remembered. What the hell was wrong with his kicking?

The noise in the hallway was growing with the crowd of freed Dionites. Noah didn't know what they thought of other prisoners, but he didn't want to stick around and find out.

He flung his whole body across the width of the corridor,

slammed shoulder first into the door. His bruised flesh flared with pain but something splintered. He stepped back again, slammed into the door once more, and this time it burst open, swinging back so fast that he ended up sprawling across the floor.

He leapt to his feet and looked over at the wall full of weapons. Sure enough most of them were gone, taken to deal with whatever was going on outside. Just as he was fearing the worst, he saw Bourne hanging from a nail in the corner.

"Howdy partner," he said, his hand closing around the familiar, comforting grip. He slid Bourne into his holster - there was climbing to be done on the way out of here, and he'd need his hands free for that. He could draw him pretty quick if there was danger.

As he turned to go he caught sight of a metal cupboard next to the door. The front was open and he could see a dozen small tubes of metal lying at the back of one of the shelves.

Bullets.

"Looks like your lucky day buddy," he said patting Bourne.

He scoured the cupboard for anything that might be the right size. He swept a handful of loose bullets into his pocket, grabbed another half-full box. Before he could think of loading Bourne he heard shouting in the corridor.

"Guards are coming!"

Noah shoved the box into a pocket of his faded combats and raced back down the prison hall, past the Dionites still battering at the cell doors. The general air of destruction told him there were other holes in the wall, but there was only one he'd seen firsthand that he knew for sure he could escape through.

OK, not for sure, but he reckoned he could manage it.

He leaped up the stairs and raced towards his cell. Who'd have thought he'd ever rush to get back to that dive? He took a moment as he passed to spit on Blood Dog's corpse, and a longer moment to say goodbye to Iver.

"Sorry, buddy," he said. "Hope it's cozy back in your universal consciousness."

Then he was at the wall. He didn't give himself time to hesitate or consider the consequences if he lost his footing. Just swung his legs out, lowered himself over the scraping edges of concrete until he was hanging out as far as he could, and then dropped.

CHAPTER 15
GOING TO TOWN

Noah's feet hit the heap of rubble at the base of the wall, the impact jarring his knees and leaving him wobbling at the top of an already unstable mound. He could feel himself slipping, and knew if he was going to fall it was always better to jump. So he flung himself sideways towards what he hoped was flat ground.

He managed to land with his hands beneath him, saving him from bashing his brains out on the road. Fire flashed through his left wrist, leaving him hoping it was only a sprain. And with so little of his body not bruised or strained already, surely it was only a matter of time before he advanced to broken bones.

"Y'know what Mama would say?" He got to his feet, patted his holster to make sure Bourne was still there. "She'd say I was lucky to have lived this far, that each bruise was a blessing from the Almighty." He turned the injured wrist, winced as the pain flared up again. "That being the case, right now I like the Almighty almost as much as I liked Blood Dog."

Running feet approached around the corner of the prison. Noah darted across the road and into the narrow gap between two houses on the opposite side of the street. He wanted many things from life right now, but being caught and locked up in that jail again wasn't one of them.

A group of Apollonian soldiers rounded the corner of the prison. One of them pointed up toward the hole in the wall through which Noah had escaped, but his commander kept him moving.

"No time," the officer yelled. "We need to get to the walls."

They disappeared again down another street.

Noah looked around. This area seemed to be quiet - hardly surprising, who'd want to live with Blood Dog and the other prisoners as neighbors? There was one hell of a noise coming from elsewhere in town though, sounds of violence and shouting. Going that way would be a last resort.

He ducked down the alley he'd been hiding in, followed it toward the walls. Here there was more noise. Some of it came from a few guards on battlements and towers taking potshots with muskets and bows, but more of it came from the right, towards the gate they'd led Noah and the chain gang out through. He followed the street until he could see what was going on, and it wasn't a pleasant sight.

The gate had been busted open, apparently blown off its hinges by another of the explosions that had hit the prison. The ground around the gate was littered with bodies, lit by torches burning in brackets above the gate. Some of the bodies wore little more than rags, like the Dionites he'd seen in the prison. A few others wore fragments of armor and the red neck scarves of Apollo's soldiers.

Soldiers stood around the gate, a few with bows, the rest with swords and clubs. Lieutenant Poulson was among them. As Noah watched, a Dionite leaped out at him from a side street. Poulson's response was expertly smooth, the blade sweeping up to block the Dionite's axe and then around to slash her across the side of the belly. She went down in a spray of blood and a tumble of falling guts.

Poulson wiped his sword and turned to his fellow soldiers.

"They must still be getting in through the west gate. Okamoto, Mason, go pick a good junction, pick them off as they come through. O'Neill, eyes out behind us. The rest of you, we've still got a gate to hold."

Was this it, Noah wondered? Had he arrived in Apollo just in time to see it fall? Not that he had any love for the place, but in a world where so much had been lost it would be a shame to see this town go the same way.

Not his concern though. He needed to get out, and that sure wasn't happening here.

He doubled back and took a narrow side street, headed toward the heart of town. He didn't like violence and it sounded like there was a hell of a lot of it up ahead, but at least if there was chaos folks might be too distracted to stop him. Remembering the guards Poulson had directed back this way, especially the young Asian woman with a glint in her eye and bow in her hand, he crossed each junction with care, wary in case an arrow should bolt out of the darkness and bring him down as just another hairy Dionite.

Soon he saw people rushing back and forth with buckets and fire hoses. It seemed the Dionites had bombed more than just the gates and the prison, setting enough charges to create chaos, alarm and the worst enemy of any city -- fire. Flames were licking the side of a tall building near the center of town, brushing the neighboring rooftops as a wild wind blew in from the north.

Noah changed course again, away from the fire fighters and on up streets of shops, most of them abandoned as people rushed to deal with the emergency. Bells were still ringing out, calling people from one area to the next or perhaps warning them of where not to go. To these people, maybe they brought order. To Noah, they were just one more element of the chaos.

At least the ringing in his own ears had subsided, though his hearing was still a little muffled. Kind of like his thinking, truth be told, busted up by lack of sleep and an excess of explosions, leaving him unable to pull together a coherent plan.

Someone moved by a shop at the junction ahead. Keeping to the shadows Noah crept forward, still wary of getting that arrow through the neck.

There was a crackle of shattering glass and the figure disappeared from view, only to reappear a minute later, arms full, standing straighter to carry her burden. Noah recognized her, framed in the light from a lantern left burning in a nearby window. It was the girl Burns had released into the ruins, the street thief with a friend in the guard. He'd seen her both inside the city and out, and he doubted any of it was on official business. Maybe she knew another way out, one not littered with dead bodies and live firing weapons.

He followed her as she crossed the junction and went down another narrow street. She disappeared around a corner and he hurried after her, giving up subtlety for speed. He rounded a building and almost ran straight onto the blade of a knife, its tip gleaming as she held it out at stomach height.

"Why you following me?" she asked in a tone that must have sounded tough to a fourteen-year-old. "You ain't with the guard."

"Whoa!" Noah raised his hands, hoped she could see the gesture in the darkness. "No need for that. I just want out of town, and I figured you probably knew the way."

She squinted at him from beneath her uneven fringe.

"I know you," she said. "You're the Dionite they caught a

few days back. You're part of this invasion."

She seemed less alarmed at the prospect than Noah might have expected, but he still didn't think it was wise to be identified as a Dionite in Apollo tonight.

"I ain't no Dionite," he said. "Just a drifter looking for the chance to keep on drifting."

"You want out of town?"

"That's right. Out of town, out of everyone's way."

She lowered the knife but kept it in her hand while she picked up the bulging sack by her feet with the other.

"What's your name drifter?" she asked.

"Noah," he replied. "Noah Brennan, from out of Tennessee."

"You sure you ain't a Dionite?"

"If I was, why would I be running away in the middle of all of this?"

She tilted her head on one side, hummed a high little tune to herself. It was near enough to familiar that Noah reckoned he could sing along, joining in with the bass notes of 'Stand By Me'.

"What you doing?" She scowled, lifted the knife again.

"Just singing along," he said. "I know that one."

"How d'you know it?"

"My Pa was a fan. How about you?"

"Molly sings it sometimes." The girl tilted her head again and her voice went serious, like he was a suspect in her interrogation room. "How's the next bit go?"

Noah sang the words this time. It was another of those crazy-ass-baboon moments, singing an old song to a juvenile thief while the town burned down around them and war raged outside the gates. But sometimes you just did what was needed to survive, and a night when that was just singing seemed to him to be a good night.

"I'm Sophie," she said as he finished the second verse.

"Sophie Mayer, out of the broken down side of broken down Apollo. And right now I want out of town too. If you can keep up then I'll show you."

And with that she was off.

CHAPTER 16
TAGGING ALONG

For all the effort he'd put into scavenging the materials from which Apollo would be built, it had never occurred to Noah to wonder where all that building was taking place. Now he was kicking himself for not considering the most obvious way out of the city.

"Why ain't the Dionites attacking here?" he asked, looking up at the half-built stretch of wall, the slabs of fresh cut stone and heaps of gathered rubble lying at its based ready to be used.

Sophie shrugged.

"Maybe they don't know about it," she replied. "Molly says the guard are careful to keep it looking tough out front even when they're expanding or repairing. Maybe they thought there'd be too many guards here. Maybe they just ain't that bright, being ignorant savages and all."

Noah thought back to Iver and the detailed medical knowledge he'd shown even in his dying moments.

"Don't reckon they're that different," he said. "Least ways not that stupid."

A couple of nervous looking sentries were pacing around on top of the wall to either side of the construction site, the drawn bows in their hands matching those on their armor. They looked around every which way, alert for any sign of

Dionites running screaming at them from the darkness. That made it easy enough for Noah and Sophie to stay concealed, talking in whispers down by the base of the wall.

"There it is." Sophie pointed to a spot halfway up the wall where chunks of worn out rock had been removed, the space held open by wooden struts while another block of the right size was fashioned nearby. "The mason working this bit cut his hand a week ago. He'll be off the job a while yet. I've been through there twice since and no-one noticed 'til they caught me outside."

It made sense. The spot was hidden from above by a mass of scaffolding, and piles of materials in the street would let you get close while staying out of most people's line of sight. It was a small enough space that no-one would think it worth guarding, but that a slim girl like Sophie could easily squeeze through.

Noah, on the other hand, might have more trouble.

"Don't suppose you know any other likely spots?" he asked.

"You think this place would still be standing if they kept leaving holes in the walls?" Sophie shook her head. "Word is the Elders are pissed enough at this hold-up. They don't like to let little things like people's injuries get in the way of their grand plans."

"Huh." Noah could tell from Sophie's tone that she considered the Elders assholes, and he'd seen nothing yet to contradict that view. But as much as they might be hindering him, these walls were pretty sturdy, and the folks in here were the best fed he'd seen since things fell apart. If you weren't busy getting thrown in jail, and if you could stomach other people for more than an hour at a time, then there were far worse places than Apollo.

Of course, that was two strikes against it for him, and he wouldn't be sorry to see the place over his shoulder and fading from view, but the world wasn't just made for the likes of Noah. Not even this broken world of ruins and rubble.

"Alright then." Noah said. "Reckon this is gonna get tight. If I get stuck can you shove me through?"

"You don't want me to go first?" Sophie asked. "I can show you the way."

"That's alright, I can manage this one on my own."

"But I'm coming with you, right?"

He'd figured this was coming - after all, she'd said she wanted out of town. Now they were here it was time to burst the girl's bubble, stop her from getting herself killed.

"Listen, you don't want to go out there tonight," he said. "Can't you hear what's happening on the other side of them walls? More fighting outside than's even going on in here, and it sure ain't pretty round the gates. What you gonna do, hide in the shadows and watch the carnage?"

"I s'pose I'm gonna do the same as you - get away from this town, with its shitty laws and its shitty fight with the shitty Dionites."

"Your Mama know you talk like that?"

"Dionites killed my Mom." Sophie crossed her arms and glared up at him. "Killed my Dad, too. So less you've got a soap clean mouth yourself you can knock off that adult knows best bullshit."

"Sorry kid." He really was, though it was hard not to laugh in the face of that indignant scowl. "Sorry 'bout your Mama and your Pa. Sorry I called you a kid for that matter. We've all been through some rough shit, and if you've made it this far then I reckon you'll carry on making it.

"But seriously, once you get past this wall and them guards and this whole mass of brutality going on out there, what you gonna do then?"

"I'm gonna come with you."

"I... you... what?"

"Said I'm coming with you, and I *reckon* you heard me just fine."

Noah glanced up at the guards. It seemed they hadn't heard them despite Sophie's voice rising in both indignation and volume. This was ridiculous.

"You can't come with me,' he said. 'I'm not a coming with me kind of guy. Where I go, I go on my own."

"Oh, like you got to this hole in the wall on your own?"

"That's different. That's asking favors, not asking to follow someone around the rest of their live-long days like a sad puppy dog."

"I ain't no sad puppy dog. I can take care of myself. I can run and hide and find ways through places. I can pick pockets, even pick locks some. I can be useful."

"There ain't no pockets out there in the wild. Ain't hardly no locks neither, and those there are, I can just smash. The rest of the world ain't like Apollo. It's a mad and dangerous place, and not one a young woman should be part of."

"Fuck you and your young woman shit. Weren't you ever young?"

"Well yeah, course I was."

"And you never had to tag along with no-one? No-one taught you what you know, how to live in this mad, dangerous world you're so keen to get back out to?"

She was right of course. Sure he hadn't been a wanderer then, but the best years of Noah's life had been spent tagging along with Jeb and Pete. First in the days before it all went to hell, following them around town as they met up with friends, shot pool, shot guns, shot the breeze over beers from the Seven Eleven. His Pa had taught him to track and hunt and tune up a car, but Jeb and Pete had taught him how to survive in the world of young men and small towns, how to swagger and to steal and to duck the authorities when the need came. They'd passed him his first smoke, bought him his first beer, rolled him his first joint. Of course, then they laughed when he coughed, sputtered, and grimaced at the taste and puked his guts up the first time he had too many. But would he have known about any of that stuff, how to fit it into his life and make a man of himself, if he hadn't been tagging along with them?

Then there'd been the aftermath.

First the aftermath of Mama's death, with Pa no more present than he'd been before and only Jeb and Pete to keep him on track. A year of what now looked like limbo, faced with a loss that rocked his own small world but not the bigger one. Getting in and out of trouble, in and out of jobs, all with Jeb and Pete showing him how to get back on his feet.

And then the real aftermath. All of them reeling at the world ripped apart, not least Jeb and Pete. But they'd still shown him how to survive, how to negotiate a place in what remained of their town. To turn his skills to survival when the lights went out. To keep himself entertained with the TV and the radio gone. To barter with neighbors for what was needed and negotiate with other townsfolk as a new order arose from the rubble of the old. He'd been tagging along with them every step of the way, only forging his own path when he didn't have a choice no more.

So, maybe Sophie was right. Maybe everybody had to tag along sometime. Maybe that was no bad thing. Maybe he even owed her for her help, owed the world for what Jeb and Pete had done for him.

But that didn't mean he was up to the job.

"Look, Sophie, I ain't saying you're wrong." He tried to look her in the eye. It was the least he could do. "Everyone's got to learn from someone. And I'd be lying if I said I wouldn't rather be roaming the roads than living with a whole mass of folks like you've got here. Maybe one day you'll choose that life too, and I hope I see you out there in the world. But I ain't the guy to show you it.

"I ain't a good man. I ain't one to stop and look after others, or to step in and help them when they need it. I've stood by and let terrible shit happen rather than put my own ass on the line. I'm a coward, and I'm selfish, and I ain't fixin' to change any time soon. The only person I ever looked after was myself. Only one who's ever tagged along with me is my gun, and it ain't done him any more good than it's done me. We both spend most of our days with empty bellies and no direction to go in, and that ain't changing anytime soon neither.

"I know you don't want to hear this, but you're still a kid. And in a place like this you get to be a kid. You get to have people look out for you, keep you in one piece, help you learn about life before it grinds you into the dirt. Folks like Sergeant Burns, your Molly, they're good for that. I admire them for it, truly I do. They make a better world while I just scrape by in the one I've got.

"And that's why I can't take you with me. Because it wouldn't be no good for me, and it sure as shit wouldn't be no good for you."

Sophie hung her head, hiding her face beneath the wild mop of her hair. Her arms were still folded across her narrow chest and she seemed to have shrunk back into herself.

"Fuck you," she muttered at last. "Hope you get stuck in the hole."

She ran off down an alley, away into the darkness.

"Reckon we deserved that," Noah said to Bourne. "And by we, I mean me, on account of you're a gun and I'm just some asshole talking to himself in the dark."

Asshole or not, it was time for action. The guards were as

far from the works as they'd been the whole time he'd stood here. He took a deep breath and hurried out of the alley, darting from a heap of rocks to a pile of pallets to a stack of bags of sand, always keeping something between him and the eye line of at least one of the soldiers.

He paused at the base of the wall, looking up to see if he'd been spotted. One of the guards was looking down into the street, and for a terrible moment Noah thought he'd been caught, but then there was a cry from the far side of the wall and the man turned away, busied himself firing arrows down into the night.

It wouldn't be much of a climb up to the hole for a man who was on the scaffolding. But for Noah, climbing up under the scaffold to stay hidden, it was a little trickier. He managed by jumping to catch the bottom edge of the opening, his fingertips scraping across rough stone. With weary arms, he heaved himself upwards, feet scrabbling against the rock wall beneath him, kicking off from any outcropping or unevenness that gave him the slightest grip. Half a minute's hauling and grunting saw him halfway up into the hole, his shoulders tight between the stones, dragging himself forward with tiny, cramped movements as he heaved the rest of his body up from behind.

"Hey!" Somebody yelled behind him, and Noah realized how terribly exposed he was, with only his ass and his frantically waggling legs to protect him from anyone behind. He wriggled forward as fast as he could.

"Hey!" The voice called out again and Noah scrambled even faster, scraping himself against the stone.

This was like his worst nightmare come true, trapped in a space so small he could barely breathe. The stones didn't just press in on his mind, they pressed in on his body, squeezing him into a passage that was nothing but blackness. What if there was nothing at the other end? What if this was all just a trick played on him by Sophie, trapping him here to die in this coffin-sized space? What if the builders had blocked up the other end? What if he died in here, enclosed, compressed, squeezed in worse than any cell or any room or any place he'd ever been in his life?

His heart was racing again, sweat breaking out across his brow.

"Hey!" Once more the voice cried out and Noah didn't know which was worse - the thought that someone was coming to catch him, or that they weren't and he was trapped in the wall all alone.

"Hey, they need us by the east gate! Things have really gone to hell."

Noah sagged with relief. The shouts weren't for him. But as he slumped, his forehead pressed against the cold stone beneath him and fear rose up once more.

"Got to get out," he muttered to Bourne, or maybe just to himself. "Got to get out. Got to get out."

He swallowed hard, pressing down the rising tide of terror, and pulled himself a few more inches through the gap. His knees were in now too, giving him another way to push forward.

"Who'd have thought the wall was this damn thick?" he said, and then, as another thought occurred to him, "Is this how Iver went mad, just muttering to himself in the dark?"

Just as he was about to panic, something cool brushed against his cheek, a breeze blowing in from the tunnel mouth. He squirmed forward a few more inches and a few more, twisted one arm around beneath him and reached out. From the elbow down it was out of the hole.

"Free!" he exclaimed joyfully, pressing that hand against the wall and dragging himself forward. His other arm emerged into the air, then his head, then his chest. Then in a rush he wriggled forward, slithering like a snake out of the hole and tumbling with a thud to the ground seven feet below. He sprawled there for a moment, face pressed against the damp earth, ass sticking up into the air, ignoring the fresh bruises and just relishing the air around him.

Free.

He was out of Apollo.

CHAPTER 17
FIGHT THE GOOD FIGHT

Not for the first time that night, Noah hauled himself up from the ground, counted his new bruises and considered himself lucky not to have suffered worse. His left wrist still felt like it was stuffed full of wire wool, but he could still feel all his fingers, so he seemed to be getting away with it for now.

He'd even gotten lucky in where the hole opened up to. Most of the wall ran over streets, but this bit was in the remains of someone's garden, and dirt was less painful than concrete. Maybe the Almighty wasn't such a bad guy after all.

He needed to get out of here before anyone spotted him, but as he started out across the open ground beneath the walls, movement caught his eye. He flung himself to the ground as a group of people came running and yelling out of the ruins.

First came an Apollonian soldier. The light from the stars and the debris belt gave her a stark appearance, the bow symbol on her chest bright white against the black of body armor, her scarf and her sword gray and angular shapes.

She turned as she came into the open, swung at one of the people following her. They were all Dionites, dressed in loincloths and wielding weapons. A small mob pursued her out of the ruins, prowling forwards with wild and bloodthirsty whoops.

The Apollonian kept backing away, trying not to get outflanked by the Dionites. But there were seven of them and only one of her. She stumbled on a patch of rubble and almost fell, swinging wildly to keep the pack from closing in, her sword ringing off their raised weapons.

As she turned to defend herself against each opponent in turn, Noah got a good look at her face. It was Sergeant Burns, with the tattoos that led to who knew where and the over eager approach with the beating stick. Sergeant Burns who'd kept quiet about his first escape attempt in return for some secrecy about her own act of kindness. Sergeant Burns whose care he'd thought he was sending Sophie back into.

There were few people here who he even halfway liked, and one of them had died in front of him less than two hours before. He was damned if he was going to let the same thing happen again.

Still lying on the ground, Noah reached around for Bourne and then for the box of ammo in his pocket. As he did so he watched the Dionites. Their way of fighting was a wild flowing way, almost acrobatic as they danced around Burns, pushing her ever backwards, darting about to avoid her blade and get themselves into better positions.

She lunged forward and hit one of them in the arm. Without armor or even clothes to protect him the sword sliced a chunk from his flesh. He leapt backwards, screaming with pain as he clutched his flapping muscle into place, trying to staunch the blood flowing from his arm.

For all the wild fluidity, there was still some kind of hierarchy among these attackers. The last Dionite to have emerged from the buildings was a well-muscled man with a towering mohawk, like a great bleached white crest rising up from the top of his head. As the injured man fell back this leader ordered others to fill the gap. There would be no reprieve, no breathing space or exit for Sergeant Burns.

Noah flipped the lid from the box of bullets, pulled the lever on Bourne that let him swing the chamber open.

The Dionites closed in tighter around her. One of them struck her arm with a club. A crack exploded through the air as the blow hit a chunk of plastic armor. Burns swung wildly as she tried to break clear of the pack surrounding her.

With a couple of bullets in hand, Noah quickly slid the first one into Bourne's chamber. There was something satisfying about actually putting bullets in the gun at last. It felt good.

Burns dived at one of the Dionites, but he dodged out of the way and as she ran past she almost collided with the remains of a brick wall. She turned, now with something to her back but no room to maneuver, nowhere left to go.

Noah turned the chamber ready to load the next bullet. Something rattled as he did it and he peered at Bourne in concern.

"Not now buddy," he muttered. "Don't go breaking on me now."

It was hard to make out details in the darkness. He prodded at the bullet he'd put in and it shifted in the chamber, rolling around a couple of millimeters' gap.

The bullets were too small.

"Shit." He tipped Bourne up, let the useless ammunition fall out.

The Dionites were getting ever closer to Burns. She lunged right with her sword, catching one of them in the leg, and then darted left. But as she swung around a club collided with the back of her forearm. Her hand spasmed and the sword fell from her grasp.

Noah dug around in his pockets, feeling for the other bullets. Maybe they'd be the right size. They hadn't come from the box, right?

He found them, dropping one as he fumbled them out of the depths of his pants. They felt bigger than the bullets from the box. Holy mother of desperation, they might actually fit.

Burns flung herself shoulder first at one of the Dionites. They fell together in the street, rolling over and over, kicking and punching and gouging, the club falling from the Dionite's hand.

Noah pressed a bullet against the hollow in Bourne's chamber. It wouldn't quite go, slid from his grasp and bounced away. He rolled another bullet from the palm of his hand, pressed this one against the chamber, hoping the problem wasn't what he thought it was.

Of course it was. These bullets were too large.

The Dionite rolled clear of Burns, reached out for his club. But she'd grabbed a brick, slammed it into his side, sent him sprawling. She staggered to her feet, even as the other Dionites circled around her again, weapons raised. The mohawked leader let out a yodeling yell, gestured for the others to close in. He had his back to Noah now, but Noah would have bet that his expression was one of of terrible, feral glee.

Noah clicked Bourne's chamber back into place, grabbed the gun by the barrel. Maybe he could use the butt as a club. Not that it had done him much good in the school library, but it was better than no weapon at all, right?

He looked at Bourne, then over at the Dionites with their long clubs and axes. One even had a spear. Maybe this wasn't much better than no weapon.

Then he saw it lying in the road, some kind of bar or narrow plank about five feet long. He leapt to his feet and ran over to it, shoving Bourne away in his holster, the useless bullets entirely abandoned. It was an old stop sign, its pole snapped off at the base and starting to rust, the sign itself scuffed and dented. He picked it up, felt the weight in his hands. He sure wouldn't have liked to be hit with it.

Of course, he didn't like to be hit at all, and attacking the Dionites wouldn't help with that. But Burns was one person ganged up on by seven, and Noah never could stand to see those kind of odds.

She was kicking and struggle, fighting with her bare hands as four of the Dionites closed in and tried to grab ahold of her. One of them staggered back with a bloody nose, and another curled over as her knee hit him in the stomach, but there were too many of them for her to fend off any longer. As they yanked her arms back, thrusting her forward into the circle of their menace, the leader stepped up, an axe raised above his head.

"Let's see your gods save you from this," he said.

It was now or never.

Noah grabbed the end of the pole with both hands, swung it back behind his shoulder. Then he ran, forcing his muscles to go as fast as they possibly could, charging for all he was worth straight towards the Dionite leader.

He let out his best impression of a deep, blood-curdling scream. It seemed like that kind of moment, and if he was fixing to die stupidly then he might as well do it in style.

The Dionites turned toward the sound, noticing him for the first time. Their leader spun around, his axe still raised, a look of confusion spreading across his face.

Noah swung the sign with all of his strength, all of his frustration, all of his anger and terror built up over the past few days. It scythed through the air. The Dionite raised a protective arm but it was too late. The stop sign slammed into the side of his neck and he was knocked to the ground in a spray of blood.

The rest of the Dionites stared down at their leader, as if

waiting for him to tell them how to respond to his defeat. He clasped one hand to the side of his neck, and with the other tried to push himself upright. But Noah had hit the jugular and blood was spraying out between his fingers in long pulses, spattering the ground, his body, the white curve of his mohawk. He looked up at Noah one last time, mouth hanging open, and then slumped down dead.

Six Dionites left, one of them injured, against Noah and Burns. He still didn't like the odds. The stop sign had been a passable weapon when he had surprise on his side, but he could hardly deflect a blow with five feet of rusted metal pipe with a blood-stained plate on the end.

One awesome moment of victory, and now the face of inevitable defeat. It had been that kind of night.

But the Dionites didn't turn on him. They didn't reorganize under a new leader. Like a pack of wild animals they stared down in numbed horror at the body of their leader then turned tail and fled, vanishing into the ruins of the old town.

"Yeah, you'd better run," Noah called after them, trying to wave the stop sign and appear more intimidating than he actually was.

Then he let the weight slip from his fingers, hitting the broken asphalt with a clang. He looked over at Burns, now freed of her grasping captors, looking almost as stunned as he felt.

"Molly, isn't it?" he said, forcing a smile. "Still reckon I'm a Dionite?"

CHAPTER 18
FIGHT OR FLIGHT

THE FUNNY THING about pain was how much you could block out while it was happening. Not that Noah hadn't noticed the scrapes and bruises he'd acquired on his way out of jail and through the wall. Not even that he'd been oblivious to the resistance of his exhausted muscles as he pushed himself, to get out of the building, out of the town, out of that gap in the wall, even to save Burns from her attackers. But on some level he'd been ignoring the exhaustion and the injuries bearing down on him.

The other funny thing about pain, about exhaustion too when push came to shove, was how much worse you could feel when you finally rested.

As Noah stood watching Burns look around for her sword, as he realized the cold gray of dawn was starting to lighten the sky, as he felt the sweet freedom of being clear of Apollo, all of that strain and pain finally caught up with him. A weariness so complete that all he could think to do was surrender.

Noah let his legs sag beneath him and sank to the ground. Sitting on a busted up road might not be comfortable, but it was a damn sight better than staying upright at the moment.

He looked over at the body of the Dionite leader, still and

silent, the blood pooled beneath him soaking into the white spikes of his hair. They darkened and wilted, turning from a bright crest to one more patch of shadow flopped across the road.

In a way he was kind of disappointed. Some small part of his brain, raised on Hanna Barbera cartoons and Quentin Tarantino movies, had expected a more spectacular result. That the edge of the stop sign would slice through the guy's neck, send his head flying on a crimson fountain. Could that happen? He didn't know if even Blood Dog had the strength, and he sure as hell didn't know the science to work it out.

Still, there was something melancholy about looking at the corpse. Not that it was Noah's first kill, just that there was always something sad about a body, whoever's it was.

Except maybe Blood Dog's. And one or two others he'd left behind, back at the start of his wandering.

He looked up, realized that Burns was looking down at him. She had her sword again, and she'd picked up the lead Dionite's axe. She was holding it out toward Noah, and he thought she might have said something.

"Sorry, what was that?" he asked.

"I said, take this." She waved the axe at him. "They need every warm body they can get at the gates."

A loud thud announced another explosion somewhere back in town. Why did it feel odd that there was still a fight to be had?

"You sure you want to be giving that to a Dionite spy?" he said.

"If you were a spy then we wouldn't be here right now," Burns replied. "Either you'd be off setting bombs or you'd have helped them take me out. No point maintaining a cover past this, especially one I never believed in."

"You believe me now?"

"Isn't that what I said?"

"Guess I wasted a whole load of effort then."

"Huh?" She was frowning at him, still waving the axe in his direction.

"I worked real hard working out how to convince you," Noah said. "I learned all sorts about Dionites. Tattoos they wear, how they're led, how they live, all kinds of stuff that ain't who I am. Even some kind of hint of what they got planned. All that strain on my brain, and I could have just waited for shit to kick off."

"Jesus you're pitiful." She shook her head. "You done feeling sorry for yourself? Because right now we've got a city to save."

"And I thought Iver was the insane one."

Noah eased himself to his feet, muscles and mind all protesting at the effort. But she was right about one thing at least – he was being pitiful, when what he should be right now was safe and clear.

"You're not going to help?" Burns glared at him. It was a glare he was getting used to, one he might even miss if he left it behind.

"In case you ain't noticed, your precious town's overrun with wild folks charging out of the woods. They've blown up the gates, blown up the jail, blown up who knows what else just this past few minutes. That's a mighty fine town you've got there, as these things go, but if it's still standing by noon then God's a kinder guy than I've been led to think."

"So what are you going to do? Just run away?"

"Not just run away. Run away hard and fast, as far as I can get with what strength you and these Dionites ain't beat out of me. And if you've got the least lick of sense you'll come with me. Find somewhere safe to live, instead of staying in some goddamn war zone."

"You lousy piece of shit." She threw the axe down on the

ground, shoved him back up against the remnants of a garage wall. "Just when I start believing you might have some decency, it turns out you're nothing but a coward.

"Run away if you want. Go hide in the woods while the world rots around you. Let everything die, if that's what kind of man you are. But this here, this is something more." She pointed towards Apollo, its walls looming over the surrounding devastation, towers rising above it like the spires of the only city left in the world. Which right about now, it maybe was. "This is the best hope there is of getting back what we once lost. This is order and safety and civilization. This is people standing by each other, not just running wild in the woods or running away whenever things get tough. We've got a hospital, you know that? You seen a hospital since the Fall? How about a school, or a college, or a workshop making new engine parts? You seen anything looks like people working together?"

"I've seen people together." Noah thought back to what he'd seen on the road, and to the way he'd been treated in the prison. The way she'd treated him. Anger flushed hot in his cheeks. "It ain't always pretty. It ain't always right. And if that's civilized then I'll take the wilds any time I'm choosing."

"No-one said it was perfect. We make mistakes, and gods know I've been trying to make less. We all have. But we started with nothing but ruin and death, and twenty years later this is what we've got. What have you achieved in that time? Walked some roads, smoked some cigarettes, used up what the dead left behind instead of trying to spend time on the living?

"You know what's out in the wilds? This is what's out in the wilds." She pointed at the Dionite lying dead beside them. "Thugs ganging up on the weak. Seven killing one. The rule of the vicious, following each other only as long as you're forced to and then it's each man for himself. The minute things got tough they turned tail and left their friend behind. Is that what you want from life?

"Course it is. Because you're a coward. And in a world where there's just one thing left worth fighting for, you'll still turn your back on it."

She strode away, back towards the gates and the sounds of struggle. Noah watched her go, sword raised but limping, angry and disheveled, and about to face her enemies on her own all over again. All that risk and effort to save her, even that amazing moment with the road sign, and she was about to get herself back into the same danger all over again. What kind of woman did that?

He sighed. The kind of woman he wanted to be around, for all the good that would do him now.

He stooped and picked up the axe. There might still be trouble out there - Dionite patrols, or stray Apollonians, or whatever wanderers and critters were drawn by the sound of violence. He'd need something to keep him safe, and a stop sign didn't seem up to the task.

His eyes drifted over to Burns again, and the town behind her. A hospital. A school. Engine parts. She was right, he'd never find those things on the road. Just more folks like this one lying dead at his feet, folks who ganged up seven to one to take down their prey, cowards and wretches even worse than him.

And in them seven on one fights, Noah the wanderer was never going to be part of the seven.

"You never know," he said, reaching down to Bourne for comfort. "They might even have bullets the right size."

In the distance, across the ruins and the woods, the hills rose higher with their promise of abandoned towns and freedom. But right here there was a town worth fighting for. And it had been twenty years since he'd had anything worth fighting for.

"Alright dammit," he called out.

He turned to follow Burns, but she'd already disappeared between the ruined buildings.

"Wait up," he shouted again.

Tiredness was still on him, but now there was determination too, something more than survival pushing him to keep going. He ran towards the buildings, hoping to catch up, the axe swinging in his hand. He rounded the corner but still couldn't see her, kept on running.

Someone stepped out of the long shadows to his left, and he turned towards them with a grin, only to see a pair of Dionites bearing down on him. There were others too, some closing in from the left, feet dislodging rubble behind, a tall woman with sharp teeth screaming orders, urging them all on.

He raised the axe. Hadn't he learned anything since he's lost Jeb and Pete? There was a reason to be cowardly, a reason to stay alone. Courage got you killed. Other people got you killed, or were the ones trying to kill you. All you had was yourself.

"Listen," he said. "I ain't with them. I'm just a wanderer, just a guy trying to get out of here."

They came closer, prowling in like wolves. Wolves with machetes and spears.

"Really. I've been in prison. I was there with Iver. You folks know Iver, right? Crazy fellow, big blond dreadlocks?"

If they knew or cared for Iver, then they weren't showing much sign of it. Just circling closer and closer while the leader raised a samurai sword and pointed it straight at him. She was like a figure out of legend, this hulking woman with her wild hair in nothing more than a loincloth and tattoos, wearing her anger like armor.

"No more walls," she growled. "No more prisons. No

more governments. No more wars. Get ready for the wild, Apollonian."

"I swear to God, I'm not..." Noah knew a lost cause when he saw one, and now that lost cause was him. Least he could do was go down fighting. He raised the axe. "For schools and hospitals and goddamn engine parts!"

It was the world's worst war cry, but he still felt it stir him as he rushed towards the leader. She stood on a mound of rubble, sword raised behind her like a hugely muscled batter at the plate. She grinned and bared her teeth.

Then the grin slumped and her whole body with it as the point of a sword appeared through her guts.

Noah stumbled to a halt as the Dionite's body fell to the ground, revealing Burns standing behind her, sword dripping with blood.

"Run, you bastards!" she yelled as the leaderless Dionites scattered.

Then she looked down at Noah.

"Well, come on," she said. "We've got a civilization to save."

CHAPTER 19
APPLIED INTELLIGENCE

"Do you even know how to use that?" Burns asked.

They crouched in the rubble a couple of hundred yards from Apollo's ruined main gates, watching the fighting. It was mostly a matter of arrows being fired back and forth, rocks and spears flung between attackers and defenders. Every so often a pack of Dionites would charge forward and get through the gateway, only to be pushed back by the massed defenders. But however the fighting went, there were still scores of Dionites between them and the gate.

"It's a sword." Noah said, looking down at the weapon he'd taken from the fallen Dionite. "Pointy end goes in, enemy falls down dead. That's about the limit of it, right?"

Burns shook her head.

"It's a Katana, one of the finest swords ever made," she said. "And it is totally wasted on you."

"What, 'cause I ain't had fancy training I can't hit someone?"

"If we get through this alive, you've got a lot to learn. Maybe if you're lucky Rasmus will teach you."

"Rasmus?"

"Lieutenant Poulson to you."

Noah thought of Poulson's scowling face and stern European tones.

"Don't reckon your Rasmus likes me much," he said.

"I'm not sure I like you much," Burns replied with a hint of a smile. "But maybe you'll grow on us."

Another Dionite attack surged toward the gate. A couple of muskets fired, sending clouds of black smoke out into the gateway. One of the Dionites fell, but the rest kept running, their war howls followed by the clash of weapons.

"Watch," Burns said.

The raid fell apart, the Dionites driven from the gate once more. As they did so, the rest fell back too, tending to the wounded, looking over to see what had been achieved.

"They're planning," Noah said. "Evaluating."

"And while they do that...?" Burns raised an eyebrow.

"They ain't attacking." Noah nodded. "So that's when we go in."

"Precisely." Burns wiped her sword with a rag on her belt, thrust it away in its sheath. "This is going to be about speed, not fighting. You ready for a sprint?"

Noah eased himself up from a crouch, keeping a chunk of wall between him and the Dionites. Just standing up made his legs ache.

"Not really," he said. "But that ain't gonna get any better. Reckon I might keep this ready."

He waved the katana through the air. Just holding such a weapon made him feel like the hero of an action film.

"Jesus." Burns shook her head. "Just try not to fall over and stab yourself, OK?" She grabbed his wrist, turned him to face the gate. "They're going for it again. Get ready."

She rose, still crouched but ready to spring into action, like an athlete at the starting line. She sure had the build for an athlete underneath all that armor and aggression.

Noah took a deep breath, tensed himself in preparation to run.

A group of Dionites rushed the gate, howling and

screaming, waving their weapons. A few arrows flew past them, a musket popped and then they were in. Noah listened to the sounds of violence, waiting for the critical moment when clashing weapons turned to footsteps, when the Dionites started to run.

"Now," Burns said as the change in tone came.

They ran toward the gate even as the Dionites ran away from it. A gap opened up between the enemy and the way into town, a safe path to salvation.

But some of the wild warriors saw them coming. Arrows and rocks hurtled toward them, and a small band of retreating Dionites turned to block their path.

Burns rushed headlong at the nearest Dionite, sidestepped to the left just as she reached him and slashed out in passing with her sword. The blow knocked the Dionite's spear aside, and the swing with which she followed it caught him across the back. Staggering away in blood and pain, the Dionite left a clear path for Noah to follow through.

Another Dionite leaped in just as Noah was almost clear. He swung the Katana but instead of hitting this new threat with samurai precision he missed the Dionite by a good half a foot. It was enough though. The man stepped back, Noah raced past, and half a minute later he was running through the gate.

He'd gotten so caught up in being on Burns' side that he hadn't given a thought to what came next. So it came as a surprise when the soldiers behind the gate raised their weapons against him.

"Whoa!" Noah cried out, realizing that to folks who'd been fighting hairy dirty wilderness tribes he probably looked an awful lot like the enemy. "I'm on your side."

"It's true," Burns said, and the weapons were lowered just enough for Noah to get past. "For now, at least."

There were a lot of soldiers crowded around the gate, with their mismatched armor, their scavenged hand weapons, and their crude muskets. Furniture had been dragged out of nearby buildings to form a barricade - tables, chairs and sideboards jumbled together in a hastily prepared defense. These people had a grim determination about them and a whole host of pointed objects.

But what became clear, as Burns led him past and further into town, was that there wasn't much depth to the defense. Past that thin emplacement of household woodwork and tired looking warriors, there were empty streets, the only movement an occasional fearful face peering out of a window.

They came to the town square, an open plaza with a well-patched floor of concrete slabs, even some flower beds around the sides. As they arrived a runner dashed in from a side street and toward the cluster of guards in the middle, just as two more dashed off in other directions. There was a frantic energy to that small group of guards, bent over a trestle table on which a map had been spread out.

"Sergeant Burns." A woman with a buzz cut and a scar on her cheek looked up as they approached. "And who by all the gods is this?"

"Noah was one of our prisoners, Captain McCloud." Burns saluted the woman. "But he helped me get clear of the Dionites. He might not look like much, but he's on our side."

"If you say so." The captain ran an incredulous eye up and down Noah.

"Hey, I can hold my own," Noah said. "I killed a man with a stop sign back there."

"Of course you did." McCloud turned back to the table. "Tell me sergeant, what did you see out there?"

Burns leaned over the map. Lanterns weighed down its four corners, but the sun itself was now high enough in the sky to show the details clearly. This had once been a map of the pre-apocalypse town, now amended with grayed out areas of ruin and a thick line marking the walls. Noah could make out what must be a prison and the town square, but beyond that he didn't know the place well enough to follow the discussion that followed.

Burns had been leading a scouting party when she got cut off from her group. She'd seen where the largest Dionite forces lay, and confirmed that large groups were still waiting to pour through if either gate fell.

"It's not just the gates now." Lieutenant Poulson, who had, until now, stood silent amid the other officers, pointed down to a stretch of wall. "They blew a hole in the wall here, where we had few defenders, and a group broke through. We're still struggling to hold it, and now we have these scum coming from behind our backs."

McCloud looked around the group.

"Thoughts, ideas?" she said. "We never expected something so thorough and coordinated. I'm open to any options, but we need to be quick."

"If I may, Captain." Rasmus bent over the map, pointed to an area in front of the main gates. "Based on Sergeant Burns" intelligence, the largest block is here. That's where they're sending assault parties out from and so where their leader must be. They are keeping us on the defensive and, as long as that happens, they will keep wearing us down. An elite strike party, supported by covering fire from the gates, could break through this rabble and take out the man or woman in charge. Take off the head and the body will fall."

"I assume you're about to volunteer to lead this party?" McCloud said.

"I am the best swordsman in the guard," Poulson said. "My leadership experience speaks for itself."

McCloud nodded.

"I can think of no-one better," she said.

The boom of another explosion shook the town.

"If they keep this up we'll have no prison left at all." McCloud pinched the bridge of her nose, stared down at the map. "Alright, Poulson. How many guards will you-"

"It won't work," Noah said, and they all turned to look at him with the very looks of challenge he'd been hoping to avoid. But he'd been learning the past few days, and if he wasn't going to use that knowledge to get out of Apollo then at least he could use it to save the place. "Dionites don't have a leader, that ain't the way they work. Least not the sort of leader who gets to set a plan and keep everyone following it through orders and structure."

"And how do you know so much about Dionites, Mr. Noah?" McCloud asked.

"He's one of them, isn't he?" Poulson said, drawing his sword. "You've brought one into our midst, Burns."

"You're the one who brought me in," Noah replied. "But I still ain't a Dionite. I just spent the last few days in the cell next to one, and he was mighty chatty if you asked him in the right kind of way."

"I said any thoughts," McCloud said, "and I stand by that, but get to the point."

"Yes ma'am." Noah placed a hand on Bourne to help settle his mind, noticed Poulson twitch his sword towards him and let go of the gun. He'd just have to do this one on his own. "Dionites ain't like you folks. Ain't no good asking who's in charge or who's the leader or what the big plan is - that ain't their way. Truth is that's probably why you've gotten to understand them so little, asking the wrong questions the wrong way.

"They live free and chaotic, an anarchist kind of deal. If they've got this organized it ain't because some leader told them to do it, it's because an idea sprang up and enough folks wanted to do it that they dragged the rest along. You take out some top leader, the rest will all keep doing what they want to do, which is attack you and maybe bust their buddies out of jail. Can't say I blame them for that bit, but there it is."

"And you have a better plan?" Poulson looked like he'd have cut Noah's head off as happily as he would a Dionite's.

"Yep." It was maybe stretching the definition of the word plan, but Noah wasn't going to let Poulson push him into backing down. Now he'd found some backbone he wanted to use it. "They may not have a big chief in charge, but most of them are still the following type, just like most folks. They fight in packs like wild animals, and like wild animals they play follow the alpha. The group that near killed Sergeant Burns here, I killed their leader and the rest up and scattered, 'cause all they wanted was to follow his lead. Same thing happened when the sergeant saved my ass, right sergeant?"

Burns nodded thoughtfully.

"It fits," she said. "I've seen them put up one hell of a struggle, and I've seen them run with only one man down."

"That's useful to know," McCloud said, "but we still need a plan."

"Oh, I've got that too," Noah said, pleased to find the pieces slotting together in his brain. "We can't chop off the head, but we can cut off one limb at a time. The groups we've seen were hunting packs, and the alpha dog always stood out. The strongest, the fanciest, even just the one giving orders. Means all you've got to do to beat any group is look for that one and deal with them. You've got shooters right, folks with muskets and bows? Spread them out among the squads. Each time they find a fight the shooter stands back, watches, and then takes down the leader. Everyone else just has to stay alive a minute or two. Without a hierarchy, there'll be no-one to stop the packs running, no second in commands to take over as those alpha dogs go down. Break enough packs and they'll lose the will to fight, or at least lose the will to keep charging your gates."

He finished talking and stood waiting to be shouted down. Instead, to his surprise, he saw several thoughtful faces turned on him and on Captain McCloud.

"Interesting." McCloud looked over to Burns. "Does this fit with what you saw?"

"Yes, Captain," Burns nodded. "Though we only got into a couple of fights, so it's hard to be certain."

"There are no certainties in war," McCloud said. "Do you vouch for this man's loyalties? If he's with them, this could all be a ruse."

This time Burns hesitated for a moment. But she looked at Noah, her mouth hitching up into a little half smile, and she nodded.

"Yes, Captain, I vouch for him."

"Very well." McCloud looked around the table. "Aside from Poulson and Noah, does anyone have any ideas?"

There was some thoughtful hemming and hawing, like a cluster of doctors assembled around an interesting disease, but McCloud didn't give it long to spread.

"Better the wrong course than no course at all." McCloud looked over at Poulson. "Rasmus, the initiative and courage behind your idea are much appreciated, but given the information behind it I'm going with Noah's plan. That said, I need someone with that initiative and courage to plug the gap in our wall and stop the packs attacking there. Take a platoon and deal with it."

"Yes, Captain." Poulson saluted, threw a final dark glare at Noah and strode away.

"We have at least one gang of the enemy inside the walls," McCloud continued. "Gods know what kind of chaos they're causing. Burns, take one of the squads patrolling near the prison and hunt them down. Take our new addition with you - he seems to have a good eye for details and for the mind of the savage, maybe he'll help you find them.

"The rest of you..."

Burns saluted and grabbed Noah's arm, dragging him off down the street.

"No need for that!" he protested. "I just got you your plan."

"And now we act on it," she said. "Follow me."

CHAPTER 20
THE HUNTING PARTY

THE PATROL THEY FOUND was small, but it held some familiar faces. Vostok laughed as Burns told him that Noah was on their side.

"I am bet you regret beating him now, yes?" he said.

The patrol also contained Lily Okamoto, the young Asian archer Noah had seen Poulson send to hold a junction earlier in the night, her comrade in that task Mason, and a red-headed woman named Ferguson.

"Well, don't this just take the biscuit," Ferguson said. "And to think we'd have shot you half a night back."

"Glad as I am you ain't doing that, shouldn't we get moving?" Noah said. "I'd like to get myself safe and supplied for the summer, don't want this place burning down before I can do it."

Vostok's group had been following the Dionites on and off for an hour, closing in so that Lily could pick one off with her bow and then pulling back before the enemy could catch them. They'd whittled away their opponents a little, and managed not to get caught. But the Dionite pack outnumbered them several times over and without Noah's insight about the alphas they'd had no way to do more than harass the enemy.

"They are spending much time around the prison," Vostok said. "Blow holes in walls, let more prisoners out, add them to group. Lily kills a few, but there are more now than at the start."

"So they're adding the prisoners?" Burns asked.

Vostok nodded.

"I think they've moved." Lily pointed down a rubble-cobbled street toward the prison. "After last time they were heading west, toward the stores."

"Let's make sure they've moved," Burns said. "I don't want any more than we can avoid getting out of jail."

"This one is enough, yes?" Vostok jerked a thumb towards Noah.

Burns put the patrol in order. Ferguson and Vostok took the lead with riot shields and clubs, looking like they could have just stepped out of a policing operation twenty years earlier. Behind them, Burns and Lilly followed, the latter with her bow at the ready, not drawn taught but with an arrow to the string as she held it in front of her. Noah and Mason took the rear, taking it in turns to look back in case any Dionites emerged from the streets behind them.

The prison loomed ahead of them, a concrete monolith rising above the surrounding houses. Its yard only stretched out to the front, and if the place had once had fences, then those had been taken away to make more space within the town walls. So as they approached the side from which Noah himself had escaped, they came straight up against the walls of the cell blocks.

Or what remained of them.

However the Dionites had arranged their explosives, they hadn't lacked imagination, ambition or ways to launch them at the upper floor. There were blackened, gaping holes all the way down the side of the building, including several amid the rubble at its base.

As they neared the road around the prison, Ferguson raised a fist and they all stopped in their tracks. She turned back, held up five fingers and then three more, and gestured down the road to the right, along the concrete wall.

Burns took a few steps back, leaned in close to Noah.

"You're the one who spotted the leaders we'd killed," she whispered. "Now it's time to see if you can identify a live one. Go take a look, see if you can work out which one's in charge."

Noah nodded.

"There any good alleys I can use to get close?" he asked.

Instead of answering Burns pointed to the building next to them, with its flat roof and fire escape up the side. She raised an eyebrow.

Noah nodded and made his way to the building, sword still in hand. The fire escape looked rusty but still intact and it didn't fall apart when he tugged tentatively at an end of the handrail. Sure, it wasn't the sturdiest thing in the world, but it would still be safer than trying to creep up on the enemy.

He climbed the stairs as quietly as he could without slowing to a crawl. Halfway up a panel creaked and began to sag beneath him. He grabbed ahold of the rail, ready to cling on for dear life, but it held steady after sinking a couple of inches, whatever had worn through apparently finding support from the other struts. Still, he moved more cautiously after that, testing each step before he took it, until a hiss and a gesture from Burns set him to hurrying again.

With a deep breath of relief, he stepped out onto the rooftop. It was littered with weeds growing in patches of wind-blown leaves and small puddles formed among the patches of mulch and roots. But there were no holes, and most importantly the far edge clearly faced straight out onto the prison.

Noah walked across the roof, crouching as he reached the

edge so as not to show himself against the bright morning sky. A couple of pigeons flapped away as he came near, and he waited a minute before peering down just in case the birds had drawn attention.

A small band of Dionites were spread along the street below, each in the same tribal style of loincloth and tattoos. Most of them were watching the surrounding streets, but two were crouched by the base of the prison wall. Noah didn't recognize the canvas bag they were fiddling around with, but if he was a gambling man, he'd have put his money on explosives.

In the middle of the Dionites stood a man with a long wooden staff and an intricate necklace of old computer cables around his neck. As Noah watched, another Dionite appeared, said something to the man with the staff and was directed by him to a position watching one of the streets.

Part of Noah wondered why these people made it so easy to spot their leaders. But then he figured that they had to know who to follow even more than Lily had to know who to shoot.

He crept back across the roof and down the fire escape, dislodging more pigeons as he made his way down. One of them seemed to glare at him before it flapped away, like it was annoyed at the human's audacity in crossing its turf. Didn't the stupid bird know this was a man-made structure?

Course that didn't make it man's world anymore.

"Spotted him," Noah said to Burns and Lily once he was back with the patrol. "Medium tall, spiky hair, carries a pole and he's wearing a necklace made out of leads and wires and shit."

"OK," Burns said. "Me, Vostok and Ferguson go into the street first but don't engage. Lily follows, takes her time, takes the leader out, then the rest of us make a racket to make sure they're scared off. If they don't scatter then we double back and make a new plan. Clear?"

"What about us?" Noah pointed towards himself and Mason.

"You keep our escape route clear."

As the others disappeared into the street outside the prison, Mason pulled a hip flask from inside his camo jacket, took a swig and waved it towards Noah.

"Hooch?" he asked.

"Hell yes." Noah tipped the flask to his lips, took a deep swig. It was like drinking sandpaper, potatoes, and ethanol. The ethanol was what counted. "Damn that's good."

He took another swig, passed the hipflask back. Voices were being raised around the corner, but they clearly hadn't reached the 'make a racket' part of the plan yet, or been charged by a screaming mob of Dionites.

"Where d'you get it?" he asked. If he was going to stick around, then being able to get a drink came high on his list of priorities.

Mason prodded his own chest with his thumb.

"You got your own distillery?" Noah asked excitedly.

Mason gave a little wobble of the head that seemed to say 'sort of' and raised the flask to his lips again.

Noah looked at him with admiration.

Behind Mason, a movement up the street caught his eye.

"Shit." He raised the sword.

A couple dozen Dionites were emerging from the side streets. As Noah and Mason looked their way they broke into a run.

Noah looked to Mason and by unspoken agreement they too both ran, fear lending them speed.

They hurtled around the corner just as Lily was drawing her bow. Noah swerved, tripped over his own feet and knocked into her. The shot went wild, over the head of the lead Dionite.

Burns turned on him, fury across her face.

"No time!" he gasped. "More coming."

He kept running straight towards the Dionites in front of them. Better the devil you knew than the one three times his size and charging after you.

The others were running too, whether because of his lead or because Mason was with him or because they too had seen what was coming. The Dionites raised their weapons ready to meet them in combat, but Noah swung his sword in a wild, wide arc and they backed up just enough for him to run on through.

If he'd meant to stay and fight it would have been a terrible move, exposing his back as he drew attention to his presence. But if he wanted to keep moving it was the best he had.

They ran on, past the bomb-planting Dionites and the leader, who raised his staff in defense but did little to stop them passing. Noah and Burns both took swipes at him as they passed, but Noah missed by a mile and Burns only scratched his arm.

It was only once they'd rounded two corners and heard no sound of pursuit that Noah stopped to catch his breath and look back.

They'd all made it out alive, which was something. But Mason was hurt, blood staining the green and brown of his sleeve, arm hanging limp by his side. There was a spatter of blood across Ferguson's cheek, though whether that was hers or someone else's was hard to tell.

"What the hell?" Burns demanded.

"There were twenty of them," Noah replied. "Appeared from nowhere behind us. I swear, we acted as soon as we saw them coming. Didn't we?"

Mason nodded. The hipflask was still in his hand, and he looked for a moment like he was about to take another swig, then thought better of it and stowed it away. Noah didn't think he'd have had the will not to drink just then, given the merest fraction of a chance.

"Appeared from nowhere, huh?" Burns stared accusingly at the bulge where Mason's hipflask had gone. Guilt clamped Noah's chest in its vice-like grip. If he hadn't had a drink would he have seen the Dionites sooner? Might he have given Lily time to take the shot?

But damn it had felt good to get a drink.

"They were letting out prisoners." Vostok shrugged. "Must have spread them out too, ready in case we come."

The *whoomp* of an explosion came from back near the prison.

"And now there's even more of them," Burns said. "Great."

"We can still do this ma'am," Lily said as she wrapped a bandage around Mason's wounded arm. She looked like a kid playing at doctors and nurses, so petite and fresh faced, Mason looking down at her like she was the sweetest thing in the whole world.

Footsteps and howling voices approached from the way they had come.

"In here." Ferguson held open the door of a nearby house. They all hurried inside and she closed the door behind them, sliding the bolt into place and peering out around the corner of a curtain.

The noises grew, footsteps approaching the house accompanied by the sound of crashing windows. Someone rattled the door handle, but when it wouldn't open they gave up. Then the window exploded in a shower of glass, Ferguson ducking back away from the flying slithers and the daylight pouring in. They all raised their weapons, ready for a desperate trapped stand, but the Dionites kept moving, the sound of them now receding on up the street. The window had been mindless destruction. Their hiding place remained intact.

"Now they really are going for the stores," Ferguson said. "No other reason to go that way."

Burns nodded. "Then we really need to stop them."

"Or what?" Noah asked. "They take a few tools, some rope, try to run off with your lumber?"

"Food," Burns said. "Old food, fresh food, recently preserved food. You think we feed a town this big without controlling those supplies? Or just by what we can scavenge? They destroy our supplies and they won't have to do this again – we'll be dead by the end of next winter."

"Well, we've still got a plan, right?" Noah said. "Only this time let's not wait long enough for any surprises."

CHAPTER 21
KILL OR BE KILLED

Noah realized as they marched down the street that he'd seen the central stores before. Not that he'd had the first idea what he was looking at, just two cylindrical towers rising up in the center of the town, but in retrospect they'd always looked a little like the granaries he'd seen out west. He wondered if they were really full of grain - precious grain that could be made into bread or porridge or best of all beer. Or was that just a good shape to be storing food in, or an easy one to build, or some kind of tradition that kept farming folks comfortable knowing that their food was still good?

It turned out that what he knew about farming couldn't even have filled Blood Dog's tiny mind. But at least he knew a little about how to fight, and he was mighty glad to be carrying a sword rather than a ploughshare.

Burns stopped them again two streets over from the stores. The Dionites seemed to be almost festive in their approach to the place, yelling and chanting and kicking up all kinds of chaos, beating their weapons against the towers to make a racket like the world's biggest tin drum.

"Noah's right," she said, and he couldn't quite read the look she gave him. "We need to do this full on or not at all. They outnumber us five to one, and Apollo's survival depends upon us.

"Lily, we won't be able to hold back and protect you. Get to a rooftop now. When we attack, look for anyone who the others are following and take them out. It may not be so blatant as them giving orders - just watch for who takes the lead. Failing that, try to stop the rest of us from getting surrounded or attacked from behind."

"Yes sir." Lily saluted and ran off between the buildings.

"Mason, you still up for this?" Burns gestured towards the blond guy's injured arm.

Mason looked around from watching Lily run off, nodded to Burns.

"Uhuh," was all he said.

"OK then, you stick with Vostok and Ferguson," Burns said "Try to find a flank you can fight if they've even got such a thing. Back up if you're getting surrounded, but press in again first chance you get. Understood?"

They all nodded. Mason took a swig from his hip flask, and this time Burns refrained from comment.

"What about me?" Noah asked.

"We've got the best job of all," Burns said, drawing her battered sword. "We're going straight for the center."

"Uh, I know I ain't no sergeant, but that sure doesn't sound like much of a plan," Noah said, imagining himself charging head-on into thirty tattooed lunatics with clubs and axes. "Won't we just get ourselves surrounded and, you know, killed?"

"Not if we do it right. We're going straight for the leader, or anyone who looks even vaguely like a leader. No hesitation, no defenses, just straight in. They've acted like wild animals so far, let's hope they stick with that. Enough scatter before us we can get straight through, chop off the head."

"I thought that's what Lily was for."

"Hopefully, yes. But are you willing to bet your life on her getting the right savage before she runs out of arrows?"

"Rather that than charge straight to my death!"

"Well tough. It's kill or be killed now - we save those stores or we settle down for a long, slow death. So, if you're with us like you say you are then you need to help me take these bastards down. And if not..."

She turned her back on him.

"If not then I'll do this alone," she said.

Noah looked down at Bourne. A gun was all very well for company and it was all he'd had for a mighty long time, but a gun didn't talk back to you, it didn't save you when you were cornered, it didn't bless you out when you were being a chicken shit coward instead of a real man. Sure, that last one might have suited some folks fine, but those folks hadn't been raised as one of the Brennan boys, or seen their brothers die just for doing what looked right.

"Here." He held the Katana out to her, took the other blade from her hand. "You know what you're doing with one of these. Me, I'll just be scaring them off long enough for you to do some real damage."

"Thanks." She smiled and took his sword.

"Just no more beatings, OK?" he said.

"Deal."

She looked around the group, catching each of their gazes in turn.

"We might not all live through this," she said. "But Apollo will. Civilization will. And that's bigger than any of us."

Once they had the Dionites in sight, Burns and Noah waited two minutes for Vostok's group to find their flank. Noah wouldn't have called it the longest two minutes of his life, not even with all the howling and banging and screaming as the Dionites tried to batter down the doors to the store with the knowledge that, if they caught sight of him, they'd come running over and maybe tear him to shreds. But he'd had more comfortable times since he came to Apollo, and that was really saying something.

"Ready?" Burns whispered at last.

"Ready," he replied.

They ran.

Not away from the Dionites this time, though that might have made a hell of a lot more sense, but straight towards them, weapons raised, Burns taking the lead. The nearest Dionite turned to them as they came, but she was too late. The Katana slashed clean through her belly and she fell to the ground in a tangle of guts and twitching limbs.

Shouts and clashing weapons announced that the other Apollonian group had found a flank to attack. Vostok's Russian battle cry was all the more fearsome for meaning nothing to Noah.

Two more Dionites ran towards them, spears held out in front of them. The thought flashed through Noah's mind that he had no idea how to reach them without getting skewered. But something else flashed past his head and one fell with an arrow through his eye. The other had just enough time to glance over in alarm before Burns had knocked his spear aside, grabbed the shaft with her spare hand and cut him down with her sword.

"That one," she said, pointing towards a Dionite woman with red tattoos and a club with old saw blades sticking out of its head.

They ran towards the Dionite, knocking others aside

rather than stopping to fight them, Noah hacking and flailing at whoever came in front of him, all the time dreading the blow that might come from behind. All they had now was momentum, and there was no point waiting for that blow. He had to trust Burns, trust Lily, trust the plan, and trust that now he didn't have other options.

The Dionite swung her club at Burns, who flung herself aside, rolling across the road and to her feet with sword raised. Noah charged in behind, screaming for all he was worth and swinging his sword. The Dionite easily dodged and swung around with her own attack.

The blow knocked his sword aside, jarring his shoulder and numbing his fingers, but he managed to keep his grip. A second blow skimmed his chest, one of the saw blades digging into his shoulder and wrenched out in a spurt of blood and ragged red pain. Noah heard more than felt himself scream.

Other Dionites were closing in. The alpha raised her club to finish off Noah.

Burns leaped. Her Katana swept down through the Dionite's arms, hacking one off and leaving the other a dangling, ragged mess. As the woman stared wide-eyed at the ruin, Burns swept the blade back up and through her neck.

The Dionite fell in a bloody heap on the ground.

Noah felt something against his back - the killing blow he had feared. Strange how it seemed softer after the saw-blade in the chest. He twisted around to at least see who had killed him, instead found a Dionite sliding to the ground, an arrow in his back, his club brushing rather than crushing Noah as he slid down dead.

He looked up at the other Dionites. They were running, the pack scattering in ones and twos down side streets.

They'd got the alpha.

He clutched at his shoulder, sank in pain to the ground. How many times today had he done this now? When did today even begin and last night end?

Burns was crouched at his side, bandages in her hand.

"It's not as bad as it looks," she said. "Probably not as bad as it feels. Messy but shallow."

She pulled out a knife, cut the sleeve from his jacket and started binding the wound with the expertise of long experience. It hurt like hell as she pulled the ragged skin into place and strapped it down, but at least the bleeding stopped.

"There." She tied off the bandage. "Get it looked at when you can - don't want it getting infected."

Noah stretched out his arm, gently at first and then with growing confidence.

"Don't even hurt so much," he said. "Thanks."

"Come on," she said. "They're not all dead. We need to chase them off for good before they find a new leader."

She held out a hand and helped him to his feet.

"Vostok?" she called out. "Ferguson?"

"Here." It was Vostok's voice, deep and eastern, but with all the solemnity a single word could carry. And when they rounded the corner to find him Noah saw why.

Vostok stood over a pair of dead Dionites, blood spattered all over him. Mason was behind him, leaning against a wall as he took the weight of an injured leg, and Lily stood in the doorway beside him, a length of pipe in her hand, her quiver empty at her side.

Ferguson lay in the street, tangled in with the Dionite bodies, her eyes staring blankly up at them.

"She got cut off," Vostok said. With one hand he was clutching a medallion that hung around his throat, a small icon of a hammer on a chain. The blood on his fingers sank into the runes engraved on it, making them stand out darkly. "I try to get through, but…"

Burns knelt down and closed Ferguson's eyes, moved her hand in a circle over the dead soldier's face. The others made the same gesture over their own chests.

"Gods guide her," Burns said.

Noah had never believed in multiple gods, wasn't sure he'd ever really believed in the single one. But as he looked down in sorrow at Ferguson's body he found himself hoping that there was something more, and that whatever it was acted kindly towards the woman who'd so briefly been his comrade in arms.

They'd been together an hour, and already he felt closer to these people than he had to anyone since Jeb and Pete. Was that another baboon-crazy-world moment, or was it just how being human worked when you had to face the worst of what life had to offer?

"We need to move." Burns rose. "Keep running them down so they can't regroup. Any of you who can run, you're with me. Anyone else head back to the town square. This isn't over yet."

Even Mason tried to come, though they soon left him behind, his injured leg slowing his run to most folks' walking speed. Noah struggled to keep up, burdened as he was by injury and exhaustion. But even with Burns and Lily racing hell for leather after the sound of the retreating Dionites, and with Vostok's long strides keeping the Russian not far behind, Noah still managed to keep them in sight.

The Dionites were running towards the edge of town, where tendrils of gray smoke were creeping up into the blue sky only to be snatched away by a rising wind. It didn't take much local knowledge to work out where they were headed – toward the gap in the wall through which they'd originally broken in, where Poulson and his soldiers had been sent to fight off any further assaults.

They reached a road running straight out towards the walls, half of the gap visible at its far end, the remnants of the pack they'd beaten milling around uncertainly in the stretch of street between them and the fighting.

Burns and the rest paused, catching their breath before they re-entered the fray. As Noah caught up, he could see two figures fighting across a heap of rubble just inside the wall. At this distance he could just make out that the Apollonian soldier might be Poulson, and he was fighting a massive Dionite with his head painted white who carried a pair of machetes.

The Dionite swung one of his blades around towards Poulson's left, then brought the other in from the other side as he parried. Noah's breath caught in his throat, certain as he was that the guardsman was a dead man.

But Poulson was better than that – better than the Dionite, better than other swordsmen, maybe better even than death. His blade whipped lightning fast, not blocking the second blow but striking the Dionite's arm, severing the muscles of his forearm so that the machete fell from his grip. Even as he took a step back, Poulson took two forwards and ran him through.

The Dionites around him turned and fled, heading down the road toward Noah and his comrades. He didn't like the idea of being over-run, even if it was by a retreat, and so he did the only thing he could think of. He threw back his head and yelled for all he was worth.

The rest of the squad joined in, shouting and screaming, Vostok banging his club against his shield. The Dionites came to a halt in the face of this aggression, mingled with the ones they'd been pursuing, looking around uncertainly as Poulson and his men started closing from the other direction.

Then something changed. Near the middle of this new, enlarged pack a voice rose up, shouting ideas, directing the Dionites into two groups. They didn't exactly form ranks, but Noah had seen nothing that looked like ranks from them through the whole night's fighting. What they did form was two large, distinct packs, each one advancing on one of the bands of soldiers, each with weapons raised and heads with them, bearing down with renewed aggression and focus.

Between them, standing on the back of an abandoned cart, was the newly emerged pack leader, a short, bald guy with a shaved head and piercings all across his face. Noah turned to Lily to point him out, then remembered that she was all out of arrows. And if Poulson's group had any ammo left, then they weren't using it, instead raising swords and spears to face the renewed onslaught.

"So much for getting them before they regrouped, huh?" Noah said.

"Different fight, same plan," Burns said. "Let's do this."

Weapons raised, the four of them advanced.

CHAPTER 22
LAST GASP

ONLY MOMENTS BEFORE the Dionites had been nothing more than a milling herd, dozens of men and women standing almost aimless in the street, without drive or direction. The effect of the new leader was electric, turning them with purpose and ferocity upon the Apollonians.

For all Burns' talk of the plan, there were no tactics this time, no maneuvers, no tricks. Just aggression and the blood pumping in their veins.

When Noah had been a kid he'd fought with quiet determination. A lot of what he'd faced had been older kids, sometimes his brothers, sometimes bullies Jeb and Pete would chase off if they turned up. That kind of fight, you did well to keep quiet, so the other guy didn't know he could make you care. If he knew that you cared, then that was halfway to winning for most bullies, and for older brothers as far as Noah could tell.

This was different.

Noah had to care. Had to care enough to keep fighting through pain and exhaustion and lost blood, through desperate odds and the fear that any moment might be his last. Had to care enough to kill folks he'd never met in his life, folks Iver might have called friends.

And so, he screamed as he attacked. Not a high-pitched,

painful, fearful scream. A deep, bellowing battle cry that touched some ancient animal part buried within his soul, that brought out his reserves of strength, turned them into raw aggression.

He screamed and he charged.

Of course the plan, if it could still be called a plan, fell apart the minute they hit the Dionites. If anyone was surprised, then it wasn't Noah. Last time they'd had the jump on them, they'd had Lily providing covering fire instead of swinging a pipe, and though they'd been outnumbered they hadn't been this outnumbered.

A pair of Dionites ran in front of him. He swung his sword, made one of them jump back and tried to charge on through the gap.

But the other Dionite dived straight at him, leaving no gap at all. They both missed with their weapons but had too much momentum to stop. They collided, bodies crashing into each other, and went sprawling onto the ground.

Noah found himself on his back, pinned down beneath a growling Dionite, kicked by a dozen different feet as the combat shifted around them. The Dionite had one hand around Noah's throat and was punching him with the other, raining blows down against his face and shoulders. Noah gave a much less warlike scream as one of the punches hit his injured shoulder, sent pain shivering down his nerves and blood oozing from the bandage. His whole left arm felt numb and heavy, leaving him barely able to lift it.

He reached up with his right hand, trying to gouge the Dionite's eyes. But the man jerked his head back and Noah just managed to scratch him along the cheek. The punching stopped as the guy grabbed Noah's wrist, but the pressure on his throat only worsened, squeezing tighter and tighter until he was gasping for air and spots danced across his vision. He felt himself sliding toward unconsciousness, and a small, treacherous part of his mind welcomed any kind of rest.

Without a free hand, he used what he had left. He jerked his leg up, smashing it into the Dionite's back. The grip loosened for a moment and Noah twisted his hand free, managed to swing a punch. As the Dionite wavered, Noah brought his knee up again and jerked his whole body, throwing the guy off of him.

Noah grabbed his sword and swept it around across the ground, cutting the Dionite's hand as he was pushing himself up. He went sprawling face first and Noah slammed an elbow into the back of his head. There was a crunch as the Dionite's nose and teeth hit the pavement. Noah hit him again, then swung the sword down to finish him off.

The fighting had passed over them while they grappled on the ground, the Dionites pushing Noah's new Apollonian friends back up the street. His instinct was to rush back and help them, but how much good could that do? They'd all still be outnumbered.

He was so used to turning his back on fights out of self-preservation, this was the first time he had felt anything like heroic.

There were a couple of Dionites between him and the new alpha. He picked up Deadweight - any weapon needed a name, and he didn't have time to give it proper thought - and ran towards them.

The first one had her back to Noah, watching something down a side street. In the hands of a proper swordsman, Deadweight might have sliced off her head or run her clean through. Wielded by Noah, the sword smacked her in the arm at an awkward angle. There was a crunch of breaking bone and a spray of blood, but the Dionite didn't go down like he'd hoped.

No time to check if she'd given up the fight. Noah

charged on up the street, once again letting out a war cry. The next Dionite looked at him with alarm, then resolve, then a bow raised and pointing straight at Noah's chest.

Noah couldn't dodge an arrow, so he did the next best thing. He flung Deadweight at the Dionite before he had time to draw back the string. Deadweight wasn't made to be thrown, and it was a lousy throw anyway, Noah losing his grip on a handle slippery with blood. But it was enough to make the Dionite dodge, pointing the bow away from Noah, and that allowed two vital seconds to close in. He shoulder barged the guy, sending him flying, and his head hit the ground with a sickening thwack.

Grabbing up the bow and arrow, Noah aimed at the Dionite alpha and fired.

It turned out he couldn't shoot a bow worth a shit. The arrow missed by at least three feet and bounced off a nearby house, snapping as it hit the street.

It still got the alpha's attention. The expression he turned on Noah was the ugliest grin he'd ever seen in his life – not just angry but leering, stretching across a face that would have looked better on a bulldog. Raising a club above his head, the alpha charged towards Noah.

Noah grabbed Deadweight, swung the blade up to block the alpha's first attack. He blocked another blow, and another, then lunged, the alpha dodging with a couple of stumbling steps.

He'd come close to hitting him that time. And those blocks – was he getting better with his sword already?

The alpha's club missed Noah by an inch as he lurched sideways away from the blow. The alpha turned to follow up on the attack, but he wasn't as quick as the others Noah had fought.

Noah almost burst out laughing. He hadn't got better with a sword – this guy was just as incompetent as him. Of course there were some attackers who weren't expert with axes or clubs or whatever they'd picked up. There were ones like Lily, archers out of arrows and forced to fight up close. And there were people better at leading than at fighting.

There were Dionites as unready for this fight as Noah was.

The realization gave him a new confidence. Instead of rushing to attack he waited for the alpha, and as he dodged the blow he turned the movement into an attack, swinging at the guy's head. Like any sane human being, especially one who wasn't much good at defending himself, the alpha ducked, just as Noah had expected. He brought Deadweight sideways and down, not quite getting the angle right but striking the alpha's head with the flat of the blade.

Reeling from the jolt, the alpha seemed to come to the same conclusion Noah had. He flung his club at Noah, forcing him to dodge, and only as he felt the alpha's shoulder slam into his gut did Noah realize that his own trick had been turned on him. The wind was knocked out of him and he was driven backwards, colliding with a wall, his head smacking against the brickwork.

Spots danced across his vision and Deadweight clanged to the ground. The alpha had a fistful of Noah's shirt in one hand and was pummeling him with the other, punching him in the stomach, the chest, the face, wherever Noah's defensive flailing wasn't.

He tried to knee the alpha in the balls, but what this guy lacked in club work skills he made up for in street brawling. He blocked Noah's leg with his own and use the movement to sweep Noah's feet out from underneath him, smashing him into the ground.

Once again, Noah found himself trapped beneath a Dionite, blows raining down upon him with growing speed and ferocity. Noah flung one arm across his face, trying to protect himself for the worst of it. With the other he tried punching the alpha, and when that made little difference, scrabbled around on the ground beside him, feeling for anything that might help him. A brick, a rock, anything more effective to hit this guy with.

His fingers closed around a slender rod with a splintered end.

Between his blurring vision and his defensive arm he could see almost nothing of what was going on. He swung blindly, putting all his strength into the attack.

The broken arrow shaft pierced the alpha's neck with a wet thunk. Blood spurted, hot and wet, down Noah's arm and all across him. It ran into his nose and mouth, making him cough and sputter and choke as he tried to get rid of the terrible taste of someone else's injury.

The alpha's growl turned into a groan and then silence as he flopped limply onto Noah.

Noah wiped the blood from his eyes. He rolled the body off of him and staggered dizzily to his feet, spitting blood and trying not to fall straight back over.

"Got him," he said, dragging the alpha's body up off the ground.

"Got him," he yelled. Though short, the alpha had been heavy with muscle and it was a struggle to lift the body and drag him up onto a cart for all to see, but Noah managed.

"Got him!" he bellowed as loud as he could.

He looked around. It had worked, or something had. All up and down the street Dionites were turning tail and running. Panic spread through the mob like ripples through water, each tiny movement adding to a greater whole that became not just one man turning or another woman running, but the whole mass rushing through the gap in the wall if they were close enough. Those that weren't were scattering into the surrounding streets, being cut down by

Apollonians as they fled.

Dropping the body, Noah sat down on the edge of the cart, finally catching his breath. Blood still dripping from him, and the taste in his mouth making him want to puke. The only piece of cloth around him not already soaked was the alpha's loincloth.

"Screw it," he muttered. Anything was better than this.

Turning away to not see what was beneath, he yanked the loincloth off the body and used it to wipe the blood from his face. It stank like the worst sort of strip club, but it was better than nothing. He flung it away when he was done.

Vostok walked up, his familiar smile back.

"Your medal, hero of the day!" the Russian said, handing Noah a canteen, slapping him hard on the shoulder and then moving on.

Gratefully, Noah took a swig of water, swilled it around and spat it out. Then he took a proper drink, only then realizing how thirsty he'd become. No wonder the world was spinning.

Burns ran up to him.

"We did it!" she exclaimed. "We did it!"

As if in a dream she grabbed Noah, leaned forward and kissed him.

Then she jerked away.

"I..." She looked confused, even cross at herself. "I didn't mean-"

Noah grabbed her arm, pulled her close and kissed her back.

"I did," he said.

Her expression was unreadable as she stood there, one hand on his shoulder, looking back into his eyes. The chaos around them, the pain and exhaustion, all seemed to fade away.

Somebody coughed.

Burns jerked away from Noah, looking to the noise in alarm.

Vostok was back and he looked serious again.

"Sergeant, it's Lily." He pointed to a nearby doorstep where the young archer sat, bow abandoned beside her, just staring at the road. "Her parents. They died fighting at the gate. I... I'm not good with..."

"The poor girl," Burns said, her worries replaced by motherly concern. "Thank you for telling me, Dimitri."

She walked over and sat down beside Lily, wrapped an arm around her and pulled her close. Lily's distant calm broke down into the most heartbreaking of sobs.

"She is a good woman, Molly," Vostok said, patting Noah's shoulder. "You break her heart and I break your neck, yes? Now come my friend, you need food and a bed. Deal with the rest later."

CHAPTER 23
AFTER THE DELUGE

WAKING UP IN A REAL BED took a little getting used to. After so many nights strapped halfway up a tree, and even a couple on a threadbare mattress with Blood Dog snoring above him, Noah felt a sense of surreality waking up under clean sheets, with a pillow beneath his head and a roof above it. But it wasn't an entirely unpleasant sort of detachment, and he lay there for a while each morning, just enjoying the moment.

Enjoying the moment was usually followed by the less enjoyable experience of coaxing his body into action. Easing movement into legs that were still stiff and aching four days after the battle. Trying not to lean on his bruises as he sat up. Feeling the twinge of his cracked rib and catching his bandages on each other as he disentangled himself from the sheets.

It was totally worth it.

This morning the sunlight warmed his skin as he shrugged off the blankets and rose reluctantly to his feet. The first thing he'd done on moving into the loft was to move the bed over next to the window, with Dimitri Vostok's help, to give him the best sense of space. He could cope with living indoors, but having a window to look out through as he fell asleep and as he rose in the morning took the experience from something to cope with into something to enjoy.

He walked over to the closet and pulled out one of his pairs of pants. That was a thing in itself, having a spare pair of pants, never mind having a closet. Of course, it was all just a passing thing, an extra pleasure while he recovered enough to get back on the road, but just because something was fleeting didn't make it worth relishing.

Like that kiss with Molly.

He paused again in front of the sink, looked at himself on the mirror. The beard was neater than he'd worn it in months, maybe years, but it still didn't fit in so well in Apollo. Was it worth shaving it off? He loved his beard, but he reckoned he'd let it go for a few more kisses like that. But what if the beard was part of his appeal? Did the famous Sergeant Burns - Lieutenant Burns now - like her men a little rough around the edges?

That thought kept him grinning as he pulled on the worn jeans and faded t-shirt that were his work clothes. Boots too - a heavy pair with steel toecaps that weren't wearing in as fast as he would have liked, and chafed despite a thick pair of socks. But like everything else, they were a lot less worn out than what he'd been wearing when he arrived in town, a lot less blood stained, and sturdier for the work ahead of him.

Washed, dressed and ready to face the world, he headed down the stairs, past other apartments and out the front door of the building. The street was quiet this early, the citizens of Apollo less bound to the routines of the wild than a wanderer like Noah was. The only ones out and about were those with special reasons to rise early. There was a guard patrol walking the streets, still on the lookout for any Dionites who had hidden out around town rather than being chased away or killed. One had killed a shopkeeper two days after the battle, leaving everyone still on edge. Aside from the guards, there were a people heading to shops or other work, and a baker's boy heading toward the walls with a tray full of bread. Noah walked along behind him, enjoying the mouthwatering smell of the new loaves.

The boy turned as he heard footsteps behind him, his face turning from fear into confusion and then to admiration as he realized that his traveling companion was not an escaped Dionite but a different sort of stranger.

"Are you Mr. Brennan?" he asked, eyes wide.

"Ain't no-one called me Mr. since before you were born," Noah replied. The kid was fourteen tops, fresh faced and gangling. "But yeah, that's me alright."

"Is it true that you bit the face off one of the savages?" the kid asked.

They fell into step together, two strangers heading in the same direction, not having to worry about whether they'd fight over the resources they found at the end. Noah couldn't quite shake off the vestige of wariness he wore like armor as he walked, but still there was something pleasant about it, about letting his guard slip a little at least.

"Bit off his whole head," he said with a grin.

The kid looked at him with wonder, almost spilled his tray as he tripped over a break in the road.

"Only kidding," Noah said. "Don't reckon no-one ever bit no-one's face off, not here, nor anywhere."

"That's not what I heard," the kid said. "They say there are savages out west worse than the ones we've got here. Men and women who'll rip off your arm just to kill you with it. Who'll roast you over a fire and save your screaming head until last."

"You ever tried roasting any critter alive?" Noah asked. "I'll tell you now, it don't stay live for long, nor screaming for that matter. If it does, then your fire ain't hot enough.

Though, if you'd even try then you ain't the sort I'd want to be talking to."

"Oh, no sir," the kid replied. "I'd never do that. I ain't no savage."

Noah looked at the kid, with his crooked glasses, his clean clothes and his skinny arms.

"I believe you," he said.

The only one there when they reached the wall was the foreman, a guy named Miguel, who Noah had already seen turn from easy going amiability to bellicose bellowing on the turn of a moment. Right now, he was in a thoughtful mood, eyeing up the piles of materials and the space still to fill in the gap.

"Yo, Brennan." Miguel grinned and tapped an imaginary watch. "What time you call this to turn up for work, huh?"

"I call it breakfast time," Noah replied.

There were already dried fruit and boiled eggs laid out on a trestle table near the work area, and the kid added his loaves to the spread. Noah didn't know how the people of Apollo distributed food supplies normally, but as long as the rebuilding went on they were distributing it at work sites. Anyone who wasn't in the hospital got fed when they turned up for the tasks assigned to them, whether that was building like Noah, baking like the kid, or patrolling like Vostok and Burns. The Council, still an abstract, distant organization to Noah, had been very clear on this - until the town was in order and the supplies checked, there would be tight controls.

He couldn't say he blamed them. These people had been through hell the past week, a lot of them had lost friends or relatives and even more had seen their homes and workplaces damaged. Any amount of order was a kind of comfort, a barrier against the chaos that had broken through their walls.

He sat and ate with Miguel, trading stories of their lives before the disaster, or the Fall as the Apollonians called it in their most ominous tones. Miguel had been a stonemason, an illegal immigrant from Mexico. Here all immigrants were welcome so long as they were willing to work, doubly so if they had a skill like his. He was the one who had injured his hand leaving the other works on the wall half finished, but Noah refrained from telling him about how that had factored in to his abandoned escape from Apollo - it wouldn't do Miguel's pride any good to know people had been coming and going through the hole he'd left.

By the time they finished the rest of the crew was turning up. They all smiled and waved at Noah, paused to say hi and check on how he was settling in. Discomfort at the attention and the mass of company got him up and working while the others were barely started on their meal, getting up high on the scaffold where he could feel the wind and get as close to alone as the work would allow. It also meant he wasn't around when an Elder stopped by to lead them in morning prayers, and for that he was grateful. These folks were welcome to believe whatever they wanted - even Miguel joined in with every sign of sincerity - but there was no way in hell Noah was drinking the Kool-Aid.

Time with people was the price he paid for food and a bed while he recuperated, but that didn't mean he had to enjoy paying that price.

"For some wandering warrior you're pretty good at this," one of the others said to him later in the morning, as they lined up the blocks and cemented them into place.

"I was never much of a warrior," Noah said.

"So you just saved us all by accident?" the man asked.

Noah laughed.

"By accident and others doing the actual saving, yeah." He spread a trowel full of cement, placed a block on the top and tapped it around until it looked straight.

"What did you do before that?" the guy asked, passing him the next block.

"Bit of building, bit engine work, bit of whatever I could before I got myself fired." Noah smiled with satisfaction as the block slotted straight into place. "It's been twenty years and one apocalypse since then, but I guess I ain't entirely forgotten how to fix up a wall."

For the second day in a row, Molly Burns' patrol came past the wall around noon and stopped there to eat lunch. And so for the second day in a row, Noah had company he cared about as he sat in the shade of the wall, wolfing down a bowl of stew and trying to ignore the stares of the rest of the crew.

"You'd have thought they ain't never seen a man eat before," he said.

"Not one who keeps half of it on his face for later." She pointed to a clump of potato hanging in his beard, where he'd spilled some of it in his rush to fill his belly. "Besides, you're not just any man. You're Noah Brennan, the mysterious stranger who turned up in the night, killed the Dionites' leader and saved us all from being murdered in our beds. At least that's what people have been telling me."

"I heard the town was saved by some gallant sergeant with a mean club swing." He rubbed at one of his older bruises, the ones she'd given him. She looked away sheepishly so he stopped, not wanting to miss the sparkle in those green eyes. "Heard she got a promotion for it too, and totally underappreciated by her peers."

"I don't know about underappreciated." She twisted her spoon around between her fingers. "Poulson did as much as me and he didn't get a promotion. I don't think he's pleased about that either."

"Screw Poulson. He was already a lieutenant and your

guard's full enough of captains already." He reached out and rested his hand on hers, not sure how she would react but not wanting to give up the chance. "You earned it. Enjoy it while it lasts."

She looked at their hands, a little smile on her face, and warmth spread through his chest and out through his body. Then she pulled her hand away and rose to her feet, done with being Molly and back to being the business-like Lieutenant Burns.

"Alright," she called out to her patrol. "Break's over, let's get going."

"See you tomorrow?" Noah asked hopefully.

She didn't quite look back, but she turned her head just enough that he could see that small smile again.

"Maybe," she said. "If we're patrolling this way."

Once she was gone Miguel ambled over, holding out a cup of water for Noah.

"Nice going esé," the foreman said. "Reckon you'll be staying with us a while longer, huh?"

"Just until I'm rested up," Noah said, looking down at his hand. "Just until I'm rested up."

CHAPTER 24
SOMETHING MORE BESIDE YOU

Drumbeats echoed around the town square, deep as a mineshaft and heavy as the loads hauled out of it. From the back of the crowd Noah watched the torches flickering at the edges of the platform, spilling out across the town square. The light made Captain McCloud's scars stand out starkly even from a distance, the ruined side of her face a mess of twitching light and shadows. Behind her sat a row of men and women in red robes and ceremonial chains, the Elders he'd been hearing so much about.

"I don't like this." Sophie stood on a crate to Noah's left, giving her enough height to see across the heads and watch what was happening. It was a hot, stale night and beads of sweat stood out against the frown that crumpled her face. "What if it was one of us?"

To Noah's other side, Molly took a deep breath, like a climber steeling herself to once more begin a difficult ascent.

"What if was one of us who had been murdered?" she said. "Wouldn't you want to see justice done?"

"I guess." Sophie didn't sound convinced, and Noah couldn't say he blamed her.

"Justice is good," he said. "But does it need to be a spectacle like this? I ain't never seen a death that left those watching any better off than they were."

"Sometimes justice has to be seen for it to work," Molly said. "It reminds us what we're fighting for. It reinforces the lessons of what we should and shouldn't do. It pleases the gods."

All through his two weeks in town Noah had been hearing about the gods. Fellow laborers with charms of Thor or Vishna or some other ancient deity around their necks. Folks who crossed themselves or crossed their fingers to ward off signs of the evil eye. Talk of ceremonies on a Sunday, though he'd managed to avoid public displays up until now. He wasn't clear on what these gods stood for or what was expected when you worshiped them, but it sure wasn't faith like his Mama had taught it.

"You really believe in all this?" he asked, looking down at Molly. "The gods and their messages and making sacrifices and all?"

She shrugged.

"I think so," she said. "I mean, it works. It's held us all together here, shown us how to keep the town together, to keep all these people alive. We've got law and order, safety in the streets, enough food to keep from starving. If it works isn't that proof enough?"

"All that proves is that folks can work together," Noah said. There was a slipperiness to her logic that he didn't like, and he wasn't convinced that she liked it much either. "I might not have seen much of that the last few years, but that don't mean it's a sign of some higher power."

A bonfire roared in front of the platform, flames creeping up through dry wood and scavenged timbers, then springing from the top so that they danced in the air, twisting patches of light and shadows across the crowd. High above the stage someone was hanging a noose over a beam, tying the rope off at the back of the stage and setting a stool beneath it. The whole scene felt like something from the westerns Noah had watched as a kid – the noose, the fire, the eager lynch mob. Except that these things had seemed fitting in the westerns, or even exciting, threats for the hero to overcome. Here they seemed bleak and menacing, shadows across the mind as well as the body.

"How do y'all know what the gods want?" Noah asked, trying to take his mind off the show before him.

"The Elders bring us insight from the Oracle," Molly said. "It's been guiding us for as long as I've been here, as long as most of us have."

"And what is this Oracle?" Noah asked "A person? A book? A movie the Elders watch on some secret projector in their basement? Bet they've got the Lion King down there too. I can picture them all sitting around the screen with their tubs of popcorn, pretending to hold solemn council sessions. Bet they all sing along with 'The Circle of Life'."

He started to sing the song himself, filling in gaps in his recollection with whatever came to mind. He hadn't watched the film since he was ten years old, and there were a lot of gaps to fill. Then as he got going, he found he was enjoying throwing nonsense in just for the hell of it.

"It's the ciiiiirrrrrcle," he yodeled, "and it steals the ball, from this bonfire in the town square to the hole in the wall."

Molly laughed.

"I used to love that tune," she said. "Not so sure anymore."

"Oh, I've got plenty more," Noah said. "You wanna hear my 'Sweet Child of Mine'? A bit of 'Walk This Way'?"

"I don't suppose you know 'Something More Beside You'?" she asked.

"Sorry," Noah said. "That don't even ring a bell."

"It was one my mom used to listen to," she said, her mouth hitching into something that was half smile and half sadness. "A country tune."

"Sorry, but if it ain't got a guitar solo then it ain't for me."

"Even 'The Circle of Life'?"

"Oh, that's got a killer lick. Most folks just forget it 'cause they get all distracted by the cartoon animals."

"What are you two going on about?" Sophie frowned down at them with all the petulance a teenager could muster.

"Life before you and the meteors," Noah said.

"Old folks are always going on about how much better things used to be," Sophie said. "I don't s'pose it could have been all that great, or you'd have found a way to keep doing that stuff."

"That's what we're trying to do here," Molly said.

"With this?" Noah pointed incredulously towards the shadow of the noose, dancing up a nearby building in the firelight.

"It's a means to an end." Molly folded her arms and stood watching the platform. People were moving about to one side, getting ready for the execution.

After a few minutes, she spoke again.

"That song, 'Something More Beside You,' that's what I think of when people ask whether I believe. I don't know that Jesus is real, or Buddha, or Allah, or any of the other stuff people use to make sense of this. I don't know if there are really gods, not like I know that I've got boots on my feet or what it feels like to go hungry. But I have to believe that there's something more besides me, besides us. That the world isn't just about people and the terrible things they do to each other. That someone will guide us out of this mess."

"Nice thing to believe," Noah said. "Reckon I'll give it a try. Hell, you teach me the song and I'll sing along."

"Are you making fun of me?" she asked.

"Not me, I swear. Even a worn out wanderer needs to find

meaning from time to time."

A group of guards emerged from beside the stage, Rasmus Poulson in the lead. Buttons gleamed on his armor and the handle of his sword at his hip. He led the way onto the platform, followed by two more guards escorting someone with their hands tied behind their back and a sack over their head. The prisoner was brought to center stage where they took their place standing on a stool, noose hanging inches from their head.

"My Mama believed in Jesus," Noah said, looking for some memory more cheerful than this spectacle. The crowd had mostly fallen silent, staring up at the stage with a terrible, mass focus. "When I was little and got scared she told me God was always watching me, looking out for me. The next couple of weeks I kept peering up at the skies, expecting to see this big bearded face looking down at me. You have any idea how hard it is to go to the can when you're eight years old and you think-"

Poulson yanked the bag off the prisoner's head and Noah abruptly fell silent.

"Are you alright?" Molly looked up at him with concern.

"I know her." Noah stared at Jen, his companion on the chain gang, her hair hacked away and her face blotchy from crying. "She's just some thief. Why are they hanging her?"

"She was one of the prisoners who escaped during the attack," Molly said. "Some of them killed a guard but no-one will admit to who did it. So the Council had them draw lots for who would be punished."

"So she's dying for something she didn't do?" Cold crept up his spine. He stiffened, his body readying itself for a fight or flight that wouldn't even be his to do.

"Maybe, maybe not," Molly said. "She was in prison for a reason, remember. And if she didn't do it then she's helping cover up for who did. There has to be justice, Noah. There has to be order."

"I guess so," Noah said. "Jesus, this is fucked up."

He looked away, unable to watch as they placed the noose around Jen's neck. But that was a coward's way out. Jen hadn't been a friend, but she was someone he'd known, someone he'd gotten along with, someone who'd suffered through many of the same things as him. The least she deserved was that he bore witness to this, whether it was justice or not.

He watched as one of the Elders stepped forward and led a prayer, inciting the crowd to join in a call for the gods to see justice done and Apollo kept safe. He watched as Poulson tightened the noose, his face showing none of the qualms that assailed Noah. But the whole time he never looked away from Jen as she stood quivering, doomed to a fate that could easily have been his. It made him sick to his stomach.

Something warm touched his hand. He looked down and saw Molly's fingers close around his, saw her look up at him with real concern.

"I'm sorry," she said.

He thought he should have smiled, should have felt reassured or happy at the touch. Maybe he did, he thought. Maybe this would have been even worse without her. But all he really felt was a hollow darkness and the approach of death.

"Let's hope there is something more," he said. "For Jen's sake at least."

"Hers and the dead guard," Molly said.

She leaned closer to him and this time he did feel something, a tingling of delight, of anticipation.

Then there was a crack as Captain McCloud kicked out the stool from underneath Jen and she fell, jerking on the end of the rope. She twitched, and a dark, damp patch spread across the front of her pants. But at least she wasn't squirming and choking. It was done.

Except that it wasn't.

The crowd waited in expectant silence until Jen fell still. Then Poulson stepped up and cut the rope, catching the body as it fell, and the whole square went wild. Shouting, stamping, cheering, singing hymns at the top of their voices and calling out praise to whoever they believed in. At a gesture from one of the Elders more guards stepped forward and helped Poulson carry the body down from the stage, towards the edge of the fire.

"What the hell?" Noah asked, and now his hand was on Bourne, not on Molly.

"Oh gods, you didn't know did you?" she said. "Oh Noah, I'm so sorry, but the gods demand sacrifices, and when there's an execution-"

He held up a hand to stop her. Didn't say anything, just watched as the body was placed on another table by the fire. An Elder stepped up and a knife flashed in the darkness, its tip glinting as it slashed down into Jen. Then the Elder held up a handful of guts and the crowd followed him in a prayer so raucous Noah couldn't even make out the words. It was like watching an animal being butchered, if that animal could talk and think and feel, if that animal were someone he'd shared meals with, shared conversation with, planned a half-assed escape with.

The tangle of guts was flung onto the fire. Then the guards grabbed Jen by her arms and legs, swung her back to get momentum, and flung her into the fire.

Though he'd never have thought it possible, Noah heard the crowd go even wilder.

"This," he said. "This is what your precious Oracle is about? What your gods demand?"

"She was going to be executed anyway," Molly said.

"Tell me you don't think that makes this right." Noah felt like his chest was being squeezed in a vice. How could people think this was acceptable? How could Molly?

She didn't answer.

Noah watched Jen burn. He didn't watch for the gods, for the Elders, for the crowd or even for Molly. It was for Jen, and for the fact that someone there shouldn't be cheering her grisly death. He didn't resist when Molly squeezed his hand again, but he didn't squeeze back.

Whatever was behind this, good or bad, gods or men, he needed to know.

He needed to know what this Oracle was about.

CHAPTER 25
OR SHOULD I GO?

"I AM TELLING YOU MY FRIENDS, this year I make it happen."

Dimitri pounded the table with his fist for emphasis, making their chipped cups bounce and the contents splash over the sides. Noah and Mason both grabbed their drinks, looking at the spillages with expressions of alarm that were only part mocking.

"This year, football tournament," Dimitri continued. "Like in days before Fall. Lift spirits. Make fun for everyone, yes?"

"Careful, Dimitri," Noah said. "We ain't got much of this to spare."

Mason nodded and held up the half empty bottle to prove a point. He wasn't telling where he'd gotten the beer from, but he'd made clear there wouldn't be more for a while. So here they were, in a little-used guard hut by the east wall, getting their drink on around an old card table.

"Alright, alright." Dimitri's blue eyes sparkled as he took a swig from his own cup, a little of the beer dribbling down the scar on his chin. "But is good idea, yes?"

Mason shrugged.

"It was a good idea last year," he said in his quiet Texan drawl. "And the year before that. And the year before that.

But you still ain't made it happen, and you ain't gonna this year. I bet my next bottle of hooch on it."

"We have football tournament." Dimitri nodded towards Noah with towering seriousness. "You see."

"He don't even mean football." Mason leaned conspiratorially towards Noah, staring out from beneath his ragged mop of dirty blond hair. "He means soccer."

"Soccer is only football!" Dimitri exclaimed. "Is when you use your foot, not pick ball up like cheating Yankee game. How you call this football, huh? Shame on you!"

He waggled a finger at both of them, leaning forward across the table. It was all Noah could do not to burst out laughing. For such a big guy Dimitri Vostok sure couldn't take his drink.

"Football, soccer, dodgeball, whatever." Noah paused for a drink. Damn it felt good to get that inside him, to feel the gentle tingle around the edges of the mind. "Just give me some goddamn entertainment. I swear, I get more pleasure singing to myself than I do from any of those shitty plays they've been putting on in the square."

"I bet you do." Dimitri winked and Mason returned the gesture.

"What's that supposed to mean?" Noah asked.

"Sergeant Burns, I think she likes old songs," Dimitri said. "I am thinking Noah Brennan knows old songs."

"Alright, yes," Noah said, "Molly likes it when I sing."

"Molly, huh?" Mason chuckled as he poured another round.

"Oh, like y'all never call her by her first name." Noah grabbed his refilled cup and hid behind his drink.

"Yes, but we never sing to her." Dimitri leaned forward, forehead furrowing into wrinkles. "But seriously, how is going with you two?"

"Ain't much of anything to go at," Noah said, sighing out

his own disappointment. "She ain't overly affectionate, and that don't give me much to work with."

"Case you ain't noticed, this ain't a town for public displays of affection." Mason sounded strangely mournful, and the others blinked at him in surprise. He shrugged. "Just sayin'."

There was a pause as they all considered what was - by the standards of that afternoon - a deep and considerable insight. Mason was right, now that Noah thought about it. Not being around people, he'd gotten used to not being around folks showing their love, or even just their idle lust. But he'd been here over a month and he wasn't sure he'd even seen a couple kissing in the street. It lent a whole extra significance to Molly taking his hand to reassure him at Jen's execution, an extra significance he hadn't known to respond to.

"Why d'you stay here Dimitri?" Noah asked. "You're a decent guy, and this place, it's kind of messed up."

"What you mean?" Dimitri leaned forward, staring intently at him. "Is good place, Apollo. Best place."

"But all these executions and sacrifices and shit." Looked into his cup for guidance. "That ain't right."

"I tell you what is not right." Dimitri rose and went to stand by the grubby window, peering out at the streets of Apollo. "Why I come to America...that is not right.

"I grow up in Moscow. Bad neighborhood. Full of gangsters. When I am twelve they try to recruit me. They use many children to carry messages, carry drugs, look out for police. They say to me 'Dimitri, it is your time now, you make plenty money working for us'. But my father, he has brought me up to be honest man, so I say no. They go away, but they still watch me.

"When I am thirteen they come again. This time they say they will hurt me if I do not join them. I say no, but they beat me badly, put me in hospital. Is not good hospital. Is poor Russian hospital for poor Russian people."

"Is that how you got your scar?" Noah asked, pointing at his chin.

Dimitri laughed.

"This? No!" he said. "This I get five years back, falling in ditch while hunting. Everybody laughs then, including me."

"It was kinda funny," Mason said. "He came rearin' up out of this hole in the ground, covered in mud and leaves and shit, lookin' like some kinda tree monster. Course we stopped laughing when we realized he was bleeding."

He poured more drinks, standing up to refill Dimitri's cup.

"When I am fourteen," the Russian continued, "they come again. By then I am growing large, like bear. Makes me more useful. They say they will hurt my father, hurt my mother, hurt my sister if I do not join them. They tell my father this, to his face.

"That night my mother packs bags, my father telephones friend in government. We get papers, get tickets, fly to America to start again. No plan, nowhere to go, just start again. We are in America three weeks when moon breaks apart and society with it.

"Where I grew up, a man who murdered became rich, became powerful, maybe became politician, while people he hurt stayed in shitty concrete flat and drank vodka and kept quiet. In Apollo, man who murders is killed and everyone sees it. There is law. There is order. There is safety. This place is not messed up, the rest of world is."

He knocked back the rest of his drink and looked out the window again. Then his face cracked into a smile.

"Noah my friend," he said, "I think is time for you to sing."

A moment later the door swung open and Molly walked

in. She looked around at the three of them. And shook her head.

"Are any of you even halfway sober?" she asked.

They looked at each other, trying and failing not to laugh.

"We ain't that bad," Noah said. "Except maybe Dimitri. Ain't that right, buddy?"

"Fuck you, Yankee," Dimitri bellowed. "I open my heart to you and get this!"

He staggered to his chair, tried to sit down and fell ass first on the concrete floor. They all laughed again.

"How'd you know we'd be here?" Noah asked.

"Mason confiscated a bottle of booze off Red Coogan on Tuesday," she said. "This is the first day off he's had since, and this is where he always goes when he thinks it's empty. Which it won't be for much longer - Poulson's got a meeting here with his sergeants in ten minutes, and he won't be impressed with any of this."

"Shit." Mason slammed the stopper back into the near-empty bottle and collected the cups.

"Come on Dimitri," he said, struggling to help the huge Russian up off the floor. "Time to get you home."

The two of them staggered out the door, Dimitri resting an arm on the top of Mason's head.

"Guess we should get going, too," Noah said.

Molly hesitated, standing just inside the doorway, looking down at the floor.

"I wanted to ask you something first," she said, quiet and hesitant.

"Rasmus ain't got a meeting here, does he?" Noah asked, narrowing his eyes.

"Yes, but we've got a little time," she said, closing the door and sitting down next to him. The old chair creaked beneath even her weight. Finally, she raised her eyes, looking straight into his. "Noah, do you think maybe you could stay? I know you've nearly finished healing, and you always said you were going to move on, but, well, maybe you could stay."

She smiled nervously, reached out to touch his hand. He looked down at those fingers, almost as care-worn as his own, but still beautiful.

"I don't know," he said. "This place, it's not me. All the people, all the noise, all that working together shit."

"The people?" she said, her smile growing. "That's your excuse? You just spent the afternoon getting drunk with those people, remember?"

"Hey, I ain't drunk!" Now it was his turn to hesitate. "OK, maybe a little. But not proper drunk."

"That's not the point."

"I know." He let out a deep sigh. "And you're right. There's people here I like. Dimitri, Mason, Sophie, even you on your better days. But there's folks like Poulson, too, and the Elders. And all this shit with the sacrifices and mystery of the Oracle. That really ain't my thing. I like to know where I stand, and for that place not to include hacking folks up for gods."

"But that's part of what keeps Apollo safe," Molly said, urgency rising in her voice. "What keeps it special. What makes us a place of order amidst this chaos."

"I get that, really I do."

He patted her hand and then rose to his feet, pacing slowly around the room with one hand on Bourne.

"Thing is, order ain't for me." He knew he meant it, but he could feel something else going on in the back of his mind. Some itch he couldn't quite scratch. Some rebellious part that didn't believe a word of it, that would accept all of this for her. It was a small part though. "At least not this much order. Not rations and work assignments and Sunday services. Not blood and death for the sake of safety. Not sacrificing a maybe innocent woman to keep the mob safe from others."

"Please, Noah." She rose and moved over to him, stood just an inch away looking up at him. "There's so much more going on here. This place is hope, hope for the future, hope for humankind. There's more going on than you've seen, more even than I've seen, and I'd explain it if I could, if I could even begin to do it justice. You can do so much good here. Please, stay for Apollo."

"For Apollo?" he asked.

"And for me," she whispered.

"If I stay," he said, "and that's a big if, but if I stay, then it's on my terms. I need to understand what I'm getting into, what I'm working towards. I need to-"

The door handle rattled. Molly stepped swiftly back away from him as the door swung open and Poulson stepped inside.

"What are you doing here, Burns?" he asked. "And what's he doing here?"

"Discussing the Dionites," she said. "But we're leaving now."

Poulson sniffed the air as Noah passed and pulled a disapproving face.

"Discussing Dionites, huh," he said.

Noah ignored him and kept on walking. He had bigger concerns than being caught drunk. He had to work out where his future lay.

CHAPTER 26
THE ELDERS

"Hey Brennan!"

Noah looked from the scaffolding to see Miguel looking up at him, hands on hips, wearing the disgruntled expression he put on whenever something interrupted his carefully ordered routine of wall repairs. That expression was very seldom turned on Noah, whose skill with bricks and stone had quickly made him one of the foreman's favorites. But today, it seemed, it was finally his fault.

"Get down here Brennan," Miguel said. "Someone wants a word with you."

He hung the cement bucket over the end of a scaffolding pole, wiped the remnants off his trowel and stowed it away in his tool belt. Miguel had given him the belt on the day they finished repairing the breach, when Noah agreed to come and join Miguel's regular crew in their repair duties. It was less dramatic work than filling a great big hole in Apollo's wall, but it was still satisfying. They were working their way slowly around the whole circle of the town's defenses, looking for areas that were damaged or weak and repairing them. There was a degree of precision demanded by the work that Noah had lost over the years, or perhaps never had when he was a young laborer, and he enjoyed sharpening his skills.

He'd made it clear at the start that this was a temporary thing, that he'd be moving on when the time came and then Miguel would need to find somebody else. The foreman had made good-natured jokes about chaining him up if he tried to leave and it was good to feel that level of appreciation, but it brought a sense of pressure as well, of responsibility towards others that he hadn't been burdened with in years.

He clambered down the scaffolding and to the street. The buildings around the area had been occupied pretty much since the Fall and been well maintained as a result. They'd also survived the Dionite attack unscathed, making this possibly the best kept part of the whole town. It made him wonder who lived here, whether people of privilege got to have the best homes or whether it was all down to opportunity and necessity. There was so much about Apollo still to work out, so much he hadn't seen.

He wasn't surprised to see that the person looking for him wore armor with the white bow and arrow symbol of Apollo. The Apollonian Guard seemed to do all of the town's official work – hunting for supplies, keeping order in the town, providing messengers between the various groups that got the work done. But as he brushed cement and brick dust from his hands he was surprised to realize who was wearing the uniform.

"Mr. Brennan." A nod of the head was as close as Captain McCloud got to saying hello. "You're to come with me to the Council Chamber. The Elders have invited you for an audience."

"Hope they're alright with meeting me dirty then," Noah said, "cause the way we're working here I don't reckon I'm gonna be clean any time soon."

Miguel shook his head but refrained from responding in front of the guard captain. Noah was sure they'd be sparring over that one later.

"That will be fine." Captain McCloud nodded up the street into town. "We don't have much formal wear in Apollo."

Falling into step beside the captain, Noah made his way up the street and toward the town square. People watched as they walked past, but Noah didn't reckon that was all about him anymore. People were starting to get over the tales of his exploits, the heroism having worn itself out when every singer in town started making up terrible tunes about his battle with the Dionite alpha. And Captain McCloud was a figure of note in her own right, powerful and respected, a leader even among the five guard captains. She answered only to the Elders, and everyone wanted to answer to them.

Everyone except Noah, at any rate.

"Did you ever serve in the armed forces, Mr. Brennan?" she asked as they walked.

"No ma'am," Noah replied. "I knew a few who went that way when they finished high school, and my pal Jimmy's pa had served in one of those fights out in the Gulf. Said it was the best and the worst decision he'd ever made. But me, I was never one for regulations and uniforms and all that saluting."

"The best and the worst." McCloud pressed her lips together, tightening the skin around some of her scars. "That sounds about right."

"What about you?" Noah asked. "Reckon you've got that air about you, if you don't mind my saying."

"I don't mind. And you're quite right. I did my time in the infantry, including a couple of tours overseas. After that, I was a private military contractor, or a mercenary as we would have been called in any honest age. I thought it was a way to carry on with the lifestyle, but it turned out I had to respect an authority to obey it, and we worked for some people it was hard to respect. People who didn't earn it."

She touched the scars on her cheek, a faraway look in her eyes.

"Were you doing that when it all went to hell?" Noah asked.

She shook her head.

"I was back home, trying to work out what to do with my life. Thirty and washed up - that's no way to be. All this chaos, all this horror, all the struggles to get by, in a perverse way it's given me back a sense of purpose."

She saluted a passing patrol as they emerged from the street and into the town square. There was a market of sorts going on, people bartering goods they'd made or scavenged. With food rationed and clothes in short supply there wasn't much of an economy in Apollo, but folks seemed to enjoy what little there was and the place was bustling.

"I asked whether you served for a reason," McCloud said. "More than one, actually. You gave a good showing in the battle and I was curious where that had come from. I'm always hoping that more people with military experience will join us, even after all these years. The Guard is important, and any injection of skills and experience is valuable. But the other reason is that you're going to have to make a choice soon, about what you are, what you want, what you're willing to fight for. And I wanted to know what sort of man was making that decision."

"Honestly, ma'am?" Noah said. "I ain't even the kid who listened in horror to Jimmy's pa's war stories. I been on my own a long time, and that ain't left me with much but selfishness and cowardice. I sure as hell ain't the guarding type."

"I think you've proved that's not true, Mr. Brennan." McCloud stopped on the steps of the Council Chamber, an old town hall with stone pillars out front and a clock at its peak that never told the time. "The question is whether you want to believe it."

She held out her hand and he shook it.

"Good luck," she said. "Whatever you choose."

He kept hold of her hand for a moment, looking her in the eye.

"What do they want from me?" he asked, suddenly suspicious of why he'd been summoned. He remembered the Elder wielding that knife on the night Jen was killed, the whole crowd chanting along with the red robed figure. An air of seriousness hanging over proceedings that set his nerves on edge.

"I imagine that they want to congratulate you," Captain McCloud said. "And to thank you. Your courage and keen observation helped to turn the tide of battle, to save civilization from the Dionites. I'm just surprised it's taken them this long to acknowledge your achievements."

She pointed toward the doors of the Chamber, a guard stood on each side.

"Just keep going straight ahead," she said. "You'll know where you're going."

With that she left.

His mind heavy with uncertainty, Noah walked up the stone steps and toward the doors.

"I've got a meeting with the Elders," he said to one of the guards.

"We know," the guard replied and pushed the door open.

Noah walked through the doorway and it slammed shut behind him. The sound echoed around a hallway tiled from floor to ceiling. It smelled old in a way almost nothing did anymore, the scent of untouched dust and stale air. People must come and go through this hallway every day and yet it somehow managed to feel like a place untouched by human footsteps, perfectly preserved while the rest of the world evolved around it, adrift in history.

He strode down the hallway, passing paneled doors to right and left. McCloud was right, he knew where he was going. It was the only place that so exalted a group as Apollo's town Elders could possibly have locked themselves away. A play of deliberate and ostentatious tradition.

At the end of the hall a pair of double doors awaited, not just paneled like those along the sides, but ornately carved with repeated abstract patterns and polished so that they shone like the mythical heartwood of some ancient forest. Framed by pillars, or at least the image of pillars, emerging from the wall and topped with a crossbeam of stone so thick and ancient looking it must have been placed there by Stone Age men. Noah was almost impressed.

A huge brass knocker hung from each door, but he ignored those. Instead, he turned the handle and pushed, the door creaking inward before him, and stepped through those doors without further summons or invitation. If the Elders wanted their guests to stand on display waiting for them, then they'd summoned the wrong guy.

They stood, a dozen men and women, mostly in ordinary clothes apart from the blue sashes around their waists, anticipating his arrival. No chains of office here, no long red robes, no grand magnificence.

There was one exception. In the middle of the group stood a short woman, her skin Indian brown. Her black haired flowed all the way to the floor, as did her long blue robes. Jewels and fragments of mirror glittered from folds of the cloth, catching the sunlight that spilled down through a round ceiling window. She held her hands wide.

"Noah, we've been waiting for you," she said.

Yet for all of her splendor Noah found his eyes drawn to something else -- a low platform in front of the Elders, a squat gray body about three feet high. Its surface was gray plastic, dotted with gaps, inlets and holes, most no larger than his finger. There were letters down one edge and a hazard sign on one corner. It sat cold and dead and gray as any other piece of machinery in the modern world.

Amongst all this grandeur, the sheer absurdity of it overwhelmed him and he burst out laughing.

"Is that a computer?" he asked.

CHAPTER 27
NOAH'S CHOICE

THE ELDERS IGNORED the question and just kept staring at Noah. The one in the long robes stepped forward around the high tech altar and stood before Noah looking up into his eyes. Her own were wide, dark pits that gleamed with a hint of madness.

"I am Sanni, Noah," she said. "I represent the Elders. The Oracle has spoken. The time has come for you to choose. The Fall has come, the ending from which the world will be reborn. You need to decide whether you stand with civilization or with the wild. Whether you will be saved with us or perish."

She spoke with deep solemnity, as if lives depended on every word. It was everything Noah had expected to find in here, yet faced with it he felt a chill run down his spine. This whole thing - Apollo, the Elders, this building - it was the beating heart of a civilization being reborn, and that sure seemed worthwhile. But there was an intensity to their gazes, a trembling in Sanni's voice that went beyond serious purpose or passion for rebuilding humanity. He shifted uncomfortably, filled with a desire to get the hell out of there.

"Ma'am, I make choices all the time," he said. "Maybe you could cut to the chase and tell me what my options are here."

"The universe does not cut to the chase, Noah," Sanni said. "It unravels slowly before us, revealing itself to us in all its wonder, unfolding the enacted will of the divine. It is a process of dawning realization, of emerging intricacy, not a race straight toward a finishing line. Patience, above so much else, is a virtue."

"I'm sure it is," Noah said. "But I ain't mighty virtuous, and I ain't inclined to standin' around waitin' on mysteries. So if you want me to think about something, maybe you could tell me what."

"You have been with us for nearly two months now," Sanni said. "Among us but not one of us. Not embracing the truth that we have seen, the light granted to us when the gods themselves sacrificed the moon so that we might be saved. Much as you are loved by the people of Apollo, this cannot continue any longer.

"The people of this town are committed to its cause. They embrace what it stands for and where it leads. Apollo is not merely a place, it is a gift from the gods, a vessel which will carry us into their bright, shining light. You must choose to be a part of that, fully part of that, taking on the role that the Oracle assigns to you, or you must leave before you taint the righteous."

So this was it. Noah had known this choice was coming, but he'd expected to face it on his own terms. And now that the time had arrived, he realized that he'd been avoiding it. He'd kept working here, living here, making friends here, the whole time avoiding turning it from something that just happened into an active decision, into being someone who decided to settle down.

Now, he had to make a decision, and that meant he had to know what would follow.

"You mentioned the role that would be assigned to me,"

he said. "So I don't get to carry on repairing the walls?"

"If you stay then you will have a higher calling," Sanni said. "The Oracle has seen your gifts – your resourcefulness, your courage, your inquiring spirit. In a matter of days, you understood the terrible threat of the Dionites better than some who have been among the righteous for years. Truly, angels guide you on your path."

"And what if they don't guide me down the path you want?" Noah said. "You want my skills, but what if I want to stay and use them in a different way?"

"That is not how Apollo works," Sanni said. "The Oracle speaks, and the gods speak through it. We merely obey. For the sake of all, everyone who stays must play the part chosen for them. There can be no exception deterring others from that for which they were chosen."

"And what have I been chosen for?" Anger grew inside him. This was what he hated about this place. Folks trying to boss him around, to tell him how to live his life. Crazies with their Oracle and their gods. This was why he'd spent so long away from people. They just weren't worth it in the end.

"You will join the guard," Sanni said. "You will keep Apollo safe and fed, maintain order and justice, protect these good people from the barbarity of a world sent to punish fallen humankind. And you will help in the search for Astra, the salvation the gods have provided."

There was no denying the appeal of being in the guard. That was where his friends worked, where Molly worked. They were the people he'd fought alongside when the Dionites attacked, and the people who arrested folks like Blood Dog. But a demand was still a demand, and Sanni's crazed ranting had him on edge, desperate to get away before the madness somehow infected him. He was on the verge of telling her where she could stick her carefully chosen role.

Until she mentioned Astra.

Iver had mentioned Astra too. It had been the hope, the dream, the thing the Dionites pinned their future on. If these folks were after it too, then maybe there was something in this Astra.

"Astra," he said. "What is it?"

"Astra is the hope of the world," Sanni said. "A place that holds the key to rebuilding civilization lost in the fall. It is out there somewhere to the north. And through obedience to the gods, we will find it. We will bring humankind through this dark time that has fallen upon us, this judgment for losing our way and our faith in the gods. We will find it, and the world will see the light again."

"If it's lost, then how do you know it's in the north?"

"The Oracle guides us."

"Yeah, right." Noah snorted derisively. "Lady, I like this town. I like the people. I like the soft beds. I like the fact that I get my belly filled regularly and it ain't all rabbit stew. But I ain't never believed in mystical oracles or none of that mumbo jumbo, and I ain't gonna start now."

Some of the Elders began muttering to each other. Sanni just smiled and waved to him to follow her, so that they both stood in front of the computer altar, looking across it at the rest of the Council.

"Would you like to see the Oracle, Noah?" she asked.

The muttering grew, Elders frowning but not challenging Sanni.

"You want me to take my orders like the other good little guards?" Noah asked. "Then yes, I do."

"You have already seen it." She held out a hand, bangles jangling on her wrist, and tapped the altar. "You stand before it right now."

Noah looked down at the gray box.

"This?" he said. "This hunk of junk is your precious

Oracle?"

Sanni pressed something on the side. There was a click, a whir, and a portion of the top of the computer shifted back. Something slid out, a block a foot across and black as any pit, yet that somehow shone with an uncanny light. On second glance, it wasn't so much a block as a sheet, thin as paper. The surface flickered with golden lines like the paths of a circuit board, splintering and growing narrower. It looked like the worst lightning storm Noah had ever seen, jagged bolts spreading and multiplying until they vanished into the consuming darkness in which they were set.

"This is the Oracle," she said.

Noah stared at it, dumbfounded, as the side facing him faded entirely to black and then flickered into movement, letters and numbers scrolling across it in a muddled, abstract mass. Twenty years. Twenty years he had been wandering the wilderness that had once been the United States of America, and in all that time he had never once seen a working computer. Not even in the homes that had generators or the towns still running small power stations after the fall. These things just did not work.

And yet this one did. Not only did it work, but it worked like nothing he had ever seen. Like something from a sci-fi movie, not a real life computer made of crude plastic with a flat screen and a keyboard.

"How?" he asked and realized he was whispering. "How does it work?"

Sanni laughed.

"Because of the gods," she said. "They left it to us as a beacon, a guide towards the future. It grants direction, wisdom, a way forward. This town was not rebuilt through the leadership of men, Noah. It was rebuilt through the miracle of the Oracle. That is why the gods must be appeased, why order must be upheld, and why we must do as it says and seek out Astra."

Noah watched, hypnotized as words appeared on the screen and then crackled to life.

"NORTH BY NORTHWEST," a voice said. An artificial voice -- tiny, metallic, and buzzing -- but clearly a woman's. "NORTH BY NORTHWEST, DISTANCE INDETERMINATE. PLEASE PROVIDE FURTHER DATA."

He took a step back needing to sit down, but there were no chairs. He needed a drink, but he had none on him, and this didn't seem like a place where that would be allowed. This was the group that kept order in Apollo, that kept it clean of drunkenness and lewd behavior just as much as it kept it clear of Dionite attacks and wolves wandering out of the wilderness.

He just stared, trying to make sense of it all. A computer. A working computer. A working computer that claimed to be a guide to some kind of salvation, some way to rebuild the world. Who knew what that might be. A bunker maybe. A secret base. A supply depot. Even some Garden of Eden set up by the gods for their loyal followers - he was so shocked he was ready to believe almost anything right now.

"Time to decide, Noah," Sanni said, squatting down beside him. She jingled as she moved, jewelry cascading up and down her arms. "What will it be? Are you with us, with the Oracle, with Apollo? Or should we turn you back out into the wild?"

CHAPTER 28
BELIEVING

Noah's hand slid down to his side, fingers resting on Bourne. The familiar feel of the gun's grip grounded him, gave him something to cling to amid the tumult in his mind.

This was insane. He'd thought he was choosing between living alone or with others, between Molly and solitude. He'd thought the choice was about him and his unbreakable defiance.

But now there was so much more to it. There was a computer, a real computer, still working decades after the rest had fallen silent. A computer with no power source, no generator or electrical grid to keep it going, feeding guidance to who knew where, with who knew what option for the future.

There was the mysterious Astra, sought by both the Apollonians and the Dionites, a mystery all its own. And he hated to leave a mystery untouched.

He rose to his feet and peered more closely at the side of the Oracle. It wasn't like any kind of computer he'd ever seen. There was no keyboard, no mouse. It didn't look like the laptops he remembered. The screen seemed to merge with the rest of the device, its shape and size changing to fit the information being displayed. There were no power sockets or inlets for cables, just a thin slot for some kind of electronic key.

He reached out and ran his fingers over that slot. He'd seen one like it once before, just after Mama died. Pa was home more then, for a little while at least. He always had work stuff with him, mostly an odd tablet computer Noah was told not to touch. But at age seventeen, forbidding something made it all the more intriguing. He'd waited a week for a chance to get hold of that tablet, to work out what was so special about it.

"You ever meet a man named Tom Brennan?" he asked.

Sanni shook her head.

"Is he a relative?" she asked.

"My father," Noah said.

"We all lost so many people." Sanni placed a hand on his shoulder. "But now we have found each other, just as we have found the gods, here in Apollo."

Noah had never really known if his father believed in God, but good people didn't say no when the pastor called round for coffee, and that distraction had given Noah his chance. He'd gone into the back room and picked up that tablet. He brushed at the screen, tapped the buttons on the side, tried anything to stir it into life. He ran his finger again and again along its key slot, sure that this must hold the answer. But it remained just a question, one more mystery around Pa's work. When he'd heard the pastor saying his goodbyes, Noah whipped out his own phone, took a photo of the tablet and the key slot, and left.

He asked around with the focused determination of a young man trying not to think about his emotional burdens, but he never did figure out what that tablet was, or see another one even remotely like it.

Until now.

Noah ran a hand across the top of the Oracle. The casing didn't have the same style of coating as his father's tablet, but that didn't mean much. His father's tablet hadn't been paper thin or glowed, but there was a similar sheen to the screen and, of course, the key slot. That was just the same and that had to mean something. Especially after what Iver had said, how he'd known a Tom Brennan, and how he'd known about Astra. There were too many connections for it to be chance. Noah didn't put much stock in chance.

He needed answers, and that meant spending time with the Oracle, exploring how it worked, finding some way to question it, not just about Astra, but about his Pa too. No way they'd let him do that here. No way he wanted to share whatever he found out with these lunatics either.

"Do you know who built this?" he asked, part curious, part playing for time while he examined the Oracle and the room around it.

"Does it matter?" Sanni said. "Whoever it was, they were ultimately guided by the gods, given a way to see us through this wilderness, this bleakness after the Fall."

"Humor me," Noah said. "Do you know? Any of you?"

He looked around at the Elders, who all shook their heads.

"It came from the gods," one of them said. "What more is there to say?"

Noah sure as hell didn't reckon this was from the gods. Probably not the government either. His Pa had always been secretive about who he worked for, but he had strong opinions on the government, opinions that didn't fit with working for them.

"Are you with us Noah?" Sanni asked. "You have seen our most holy of treasures. You have born witness to the Oracle, that which will guide us back to the light. You have heard what it has planned for you in our town. Will you stay with us? Will you help us find Astra?"

It was so much to process, so much to take in. The Oracle itself, a piece of technology that would have been strange even before the rest died. The link to his father, who might still be out there somewhere, alive and connected into whatever this was. The consequences for the people he knew, people like Molly and Dimitri, that they were being led not by mere superstition but by technology, by knowledge, by some kind of guide to humanity's survival. A guide their enemies wanted so badly that they'd tried to storm the town for it. If they both wanted Astra, then surely that was what the assault had been about, what Ferguson had died for?

He didn't know that he wanted to stay - the lies, the strange technologically led religion, the plans they had to dictate his future...that was all too much. But he couldn't leave, not now, not until he knew more.

Not until he'd found a way to get ahold of the Oracle, to get it away from these lunatics and put it to better use. Like finding his father.

"Reckon I will," he said.

"In a month's time the Hand of Apollo will come," Sanni said. "Then you will be baptized. You will become one of us."

She smiled, a wide, gaping smile to match the strange gleam in her eyes.

Noah smiled back, but his attention wasn't on Sanni. It was on the placement of windows around the room, the distance from the Oracle to the door, the way the Oracle bent when Sanni picked it up meaning maybe it could be rolled up and stowed in a bag for an easy getaway.

"Lookin' forward to it," he said.

As he walked out of the Council Chamber, he paused at the top of the steps and rested his hand on Bourne. He looked out across Apollo, at the people, the buildings, the bustle of life. Then he looked up into the sky at the bright band glowing in the south as dusk closed in, a band that had once been the moon before the world fell apart and places like Apollo arose from its ashes. A place that might be civilization reborn, or might just be a dozen crazies praying to a computer. But at least it was a place more comfortable than wandering the wilds.

"Looks like we've found a place to stay, buddy," he said, patting Bourne. "Now we just need a plan."

I HOPE YOU ENJOYED THE APOCALYPSE.

Be the first to know when the next book comes out.
Head over to www.AGWyattAuthor.com
and sign up for my free newsletter.

Printed in Great Britain
by Amazon